Jane felt co
alone with

"And this Mount Lavinia," he asked, "it, too, pleases you?"

"It enchants me," Jane answered.

"Then you must have a memento of it." He reached in his pocket to withdraw, unwrapped, a string of bean beads. A simple string, yet the only adornment for the simple cotton dress she wore. Her hands went instinctively to her throat and she felt her cheeks burning.

"I think," he said softly, "that these will be right, little one. May I?" Without waiting for her permission, he put his long, sensitive, olive-skinned hands around her neck and fastened the clasp of the necklet carefully. His fingers were cool...yet warm. But his touch, even after he'd removed his hands, tingled her skin.

JOYCE DINGWELL
is also the author of these
Harlequin Romances

Many of these titles are available at your local bookseller.

For a free catalogue listing all available Harlequin Romances
and Harlequin Presents, send your name and address to:

HARLEQUIN READER SERVICE
1440 South Priest Drive, Tempe, AZ 85281
Canadian address: Stratford, Ontario N5A 6W2

I and My Heart

by

JOYCE DINGWELL

Harlequin Books

TORONTO • LONDON • LOS ANGELES • AMSTERDAM
SYDNEY • HAMBURG • PARIS • STOCKHOLM • ATHENS • TOKYO

Original hardcover edition published in 1967
by Mills & Boon Limited

ISBN 0-373-01452-X

Harlequin edition published December 1970
Second printing August 1981

Printed in Canada

CHAPTER ONE

IT had been different in the assembly hall when Mr. Lennox had handed Jane the award.

Handomsely engraved, with many curlicues, swirls and touches of gold, it had announced that this year's star pupil in the Ackland School for Advertising was J. Winter.

Mr. Lennox had read out the citation, re-rolled the scroll, then handed it . . . with the envelope . . . to Jane.

There had been applause.

On top of the world, her mind scurrying in a million directions – and none, Jane had answered to Mr. Lennox's kindly, 'What next, my dear?' a fervant, 'Overseas, of course!'

'It's only two hundred dollars,' Mr. Lennox had reminded her of the contents of the envelope, to which Jane had said, 'It's my beginning, now I can do the rest.'

Over coffee afterwards, her fellow students milling around her to offer their congratulations, Jane had still known wings. When she had done the Ackland test paper . . . this year it had been an advertisement for selling engagement rings . . . she had felt her effort was good. But never, she had thought, *that* good. Award-good. Two hundred dollars good.

As she had sat in the examination room biting her pen she had remembered a newspaper her half-sister had sent from Colombo . . . the *Sinhalese Observer* was printed in English . . . and how interested she had been in the matrimonial advertisements – horoscopes to be interchanged, dowries to be stated.

She had begun her advertisement: 'I am Aquarius and I offer Fifty Rupees . . .' and from that had proceeded to western troths of diamonds and platinum at much more than fifty rupees.

Mr. Lennox, in the citation, had praised her for adopting such a novel approach, and Jane had thought a little wryly that for the first time in her life April, if unconsciously, had done her a good turn.

However, it had not been the time to be ungenerous, it had been smiling time, top of the world time.

But of course the coffee and praise had finished. Mr. Lennox had gone back to his office. The class had gone home. And among them, Jane. On the top of the bus, naturally on top when she was in these elevated spirits, Jane had started out in triumph. Only the elevation hadn't lasted. Not even for two stops.

Jane had come back to earth.

Most certainly, she realized, she could not go overseas, nor anywhere much. As Mr. Lennox had said the sum of two hundred dollars, one hundred pounds, was insufficient. And she had nothing more. The rest had gone to April.

'Janey,' her mother had said ... how often had Mother drawn a breath and started the bad news, for Jane, like that?

'Yes, Mother?'

'It's April, darling. We must give April her chance. That voice – that lovely voice—'

Once it had been April's health, actually superb, and once it had been a love affair that had never really been on. Had April's voice been as ephemeral, Jane might have rebelled at last, but the fact was that her half-sister April *did* have a voice, how good, Jane, a lover but never an authority on music, did not know, but appealing enough, and perhaps promising enough as well.

'Jane, we must give April her chance.'

Jane had known what her mother had meant. There

had been a nest egg left for Jane by her mother's second husband and Jane's father, only a small sum, but handy. It would have been very handy, with her two hundred dollars, now.

But it was gone. Gone with April. Gone to England where April was to have her chance. If April had taken her chance less luxuriously, tourist class instead of first, a less fabulous wardrobe, there might still have been something to supplement the award. But there was nothing at all. If her mother's money had not been paid weekly there would have been none of that.

'I can't help it, Jane,' Mrs. Winter had defended plaintively, 'not with my paradise bird. Don't think I love my two daughters any differently, darling, but you are my little brown wren.'

She had been wrong there in one instance. It had been the loving differently, for Jane was well aware that she was indeed a brown wren – compared to April, anyway, April of the flame red hair and the turquoise eyes. Jane was acorn, three acorn freckles on the small, rather undecided nose. No coral wash on perfectly moulded cheeks, just fair skin. No full red mouth. Just a wren.

But the not loving any differently, that *had* been wrong. Never had Mother loved Jane as she loved April.

For one reason, April had been Vernon's child, and Vernon, the girls' mother had admitted had been her dear, dear love.

'Just like in books,' she had related often, 'it was a whirlwind romance, and it lasted only as long. April was just born when Vernie, darling Vernie, died.

'Lots of people were astounded when I married Paul Winter so soon. But I was very young, very lonely, and I thought that Paul—'

Her voice had always trailed away at this juncture, but you gather that she had relied on Paul to keep and cherish her, not just to give her another daughter, then die, too.

For the second husband had done just that, died leaving only a small income to his wife and a nest egg ... now gone to April ... for Jane.

'He was a good man,' Jane's mother had assured her, 'but you must understand, little brown wren, that there's only one real love.'

Mrs. Winter was given to such romanticisms, something that cool-headed April was not, which made Jane think that April took after her father, Vernon Winthrop, though in looks April's and Jane's mother certainly hoped her elder daughter took after her. Who could question such a fervent hope? Not when one was claiming a paradise bird.

There was only a year between them, between April and Jane. And a wide, wide world

When they had been young Mrs. Winter had used April's seniority as an excuse for favours – 'April first, little wren, she's older than you.' – but after they had been nineteen and eighteen, she had dropped the pretence.

'Jane, we must give April her chance.'

All this came to Jane now as she sat on the top deck of the bus and realized, as her spirits plummeted, that she shouldn't have climbed the stairs, that the lower level was more in keeping.

Yet perhaps, she thought, she could keep the hundred pounds secret. After all, it wasn't being selfish, she could buy Mother something except that Mother wanted nothing except something for April. But I'll still keep it quiet, determined Jane. Mother takes no interest in any of my friends, she need never know from them.

She opened the paper she had bought, wondering wistfully, for she always had longed to see England, how it would be to sit in the top deck of a bus in London and open a paper, which, if she could only augment what she had in her envelope by careful budgeting, by extra work, she might be able to do even yet. The thought brought back some of the elevation.

Then she saw it. Only on a slack news night would the papers have bothered to feature it.

Miss Jane Winter . . . 'I am Aquarius' . . . offers Fifty Rupees and wins Two Hundred Dollars.

'Oh, no!' said Jane.

She slipped the paper down behind the seat and stared out at the slowly darkling streets. As she got off the bus she thought hopefully that she still might escape . . . escape, how silly she was being, wasn't she twenty-one now, an adult with a mind of her own? . . . for her mother's intimate friends were like her mother, card devotees, practically non-readers, they probably would never see the item, pass it on.

It's deceitful, she thought, but I can't . . . I won't . . . keep on helping April. She turned in at the block of flats.

Usually Mother was playing bridge upstairs, or, if there was no fourth available, sitting under the lamp trying her hand at solitaire. But tonight Mrs. Winter opened the door. There was sherry on the table and two excited pink spots on her mother's cheeks. If Jane had looked closer she would have seen there was an aerogramme in her mother's hand. But Jane's eyes were roving around for a newspaper.

'Darling little wren,' said Mrs. Winter at once, 'I just happened to turn on the radio, and there you were! Jane – my Jane! The Ackland Award! Two hundred dollars! One hundred pounds!'

'And a scroll,' Jane said dully; she felt dull. But she held out the citation.

'Of course, pet.' Mrs. Winter did not even glance at it. 'Oh, I'm so proud!'

9

She was pouring the sherry now . . . fussing, praising, telling Jane she always knew she would make good, dear Paul had been similarly talented, words had come easily, too, to him, and only that he had died so soon . . .

It went on and on, the story Jane knew so well through repetition. It left her father Paul to concentrate on her mother. How it would have been hard enough to bring up *one* fatherless child, but when it came to two . . .

'And the first such a child as April. I mean, my wren, just one look at her and you know she must have her chance.'

Fleetingly Jane thought of Jeff . . . Jane was to have married Jeff, only suddenly April had been interested, so had been given her chance. She had lost her interest, of course, and returned Jeff to Jane, only Jane had lost interest, too.

'April is something that doesn't happen very often, darling,' her mother was babbling, 'I know you understand, wren.'

'Mother,' interrupted Jane, suddenly aware that something was going to be disclosed, 'what is this?'

As Mrs. Winter, at a loss for once, could find no immediate words, Jane reminded her, 'She has enough money to start her off in London.'

'But, darling, she's not in London.'

'She will be next week.'

'But she won't, Jane. You see, the naughty girl got off at Colombo. Oh, dear, it's very dreadful of her, but' – the pink spots quite red now – 'a wonderful chance.'

'For what? Is there a musical opening in Ceylon?'

'Not musical, darling, but matrimonial. April – well, April has an offer.'

Quite stupidly Jane asked again, 'For what?'

'I told you, dear – marriage. April doesn't say so in bare words, but – well, read it for yourself.'

The letter that Jane had not seen in her mother's hand

was put in her own hand. Certainly there were no *bare* words.

This man her half-sister had met had tremendous possibilities ... he was a Portuguese trader and exporter, as charming and as rich as you could dream. He had fallen in love with her, and April was quite sure she was in love with him. Yes, remembered Jane, as April had been sure at first with Jeff. Only there was an obstacle. The Portuguese were very formal. Not darling Rodriguez, of course, but it appeared he had a strict uncle ...

Rodriguez had suggested that if April could bring over one of her family it might make a good impression ... especially with a representative like Jane, April had written on her own account, quiet, respectable. Jane added, 'dull.'

'When I read the letter I burst into tears,' admitted Mrs. Winter. 'How, I thought, can Jane go? I have a little put aside, but very little, Jane has a little, but very little, and both put together is still not enough, and then just by chance I put on the news, and darling, darling wren—'

'I'm not going.' Jane broke this in rather heatedly for her; she was usually a calm person. 'I'm using the money for further study. I'm – I'm—'

'The news spoke about how you based your winning paper on April's *Sinhalese Observer*. Quite clever of you, Jane, though the real credit must go to April.'

On it went. On. On.

It wasn't as though Jane was being asked to *give* the money to April, why, she was to have the pleasure of it herself. Then there was nothing to stop Jane, after she had made her appearance, done her duty, of going on to London. Mrs. Winter spoke hurriedly of this in case Jane interrupted, 'On what?'

'Then, who knows,' finished Mrs. Winter triumphantly, 'you mightn't go on at all. April might find you somebody suitable, in a position like she would have once she married this man that would be easy.'

Yes, some under-clerk would suit Jane . . . and April . . quite well.

'I'm not going,' Jane said again.

'Darling, your own sister—'

'No.'

'Our paradise bird—'

'No, Mother.'

'But, Jane, we must give April her chance.'

Give April her chance . . . give April her chance . . . .
Tossing in bed that night, Jane heard nothing else, even the traffic boomed it, the bedside clock ticked it. Give April her chance.

Well, she supposed wearily at last, at least, as Mother pointed out, *I* will be using the money, and it's the first time I'll ever have done that.

Then if I still hold out, don't agree to go, will I use the money at all? She saw it eking away, in cablegrams of regret, in compensating presents, in endless correspondence with something as well as words tucked within the envelopes, and all done with sighs, ahs, dabs to eyes and reproachful looks.

Oh, what was the use?

Colombo, Jane tasted next. It sounded interesting enough. But just interesting, though, simply places faraway, never – never London. Still, it could be a beginning, one could always go on from there, if one raised the extra money, if one didn't fall to the attraction of that under-clerk that April might produce. In the darkness Jane gave a wry smile. But she knew . . . defeatedly . . . there was no other way out, no alternative. It was either Ceylon for her, or nothing. She had been a brown wren too long not to recognize that.

In which case she would not prolong the misery, neither Mother's, nor her's. She came out to breakfast and forestalled her mother's pathetic, 'Wren darling—' with a resigned, 'All right, I'll go.'

'Jane, you mean it?'

'I've just said so.'

'You're so sweet, so reliable. Just like Paul, your dear father, except that I could never, well—' A sigh. 'And I'm sure you will be just what April needs, someone quiet, respectable—'

'Dull.'

'Well, we all can't be paradise birds, and you will have the satisfaction of knowing you've given April her chance.'

Yes, her chance. Jane put down the cup she had taken up and went to the window. It was a rather poor flat with a very indifferent view, but with money spent regularly on April there had been little choice.

For a moment Jane wondered about her mother. *She* lived in this poor flat, too. She looked tenderly at her ... and wistfully. With the money she would have to put out on getting to Ceylon the two of them ...

But Mrs. Winter's eyes were shining now, she did not care about views, only April's view. View – to what?

'A wonderful chance,' she was purring.

The moment of tenderness left Jane. There was something terribly mercenary in planning to settle an affair in such a deliberate way as this.

'You'll be very circumspect, Jane ... but as though you could be anything else ... it's just, darling, that sometimes even the most reticent of girls change when they leave their home for a foreign country, and in a case like this—'

'Of giving April her chance, you mean? That kind of case?'

'Yes, darling.' Mrs. Winter's eyes were a little puzzled as they rested on Jane.

'Don't worry, Mother.' But Jane said it abstractedly.

Give April her chance. The message was ringing in her again. Give April her chance. But who, she wondered bleakly, would give Jane hers?

For a rather frail woman, or so her mother always had implied, suddenly Mrs. Winter changed to a dynamo. Pushing aside her cards that were never removed from the table, she sat down and leafed over the telephone directory.

'It will have to be air, of course, dear, ships take too long.'

'They're cheaper.' As she answered Jane remembered April's luxury suite on the *Fairhaven* which had been dearer.

Mrs. Winter was frowning slightly. Cheapness, when it was not for April, rather attracted her. However, there was the time factor to be considered: time, according to April's letter, *mattered*. 'Make her come, Mummy,' April had written. She had sounded in haste. Even if Jane managed a ship berth immediately she still could not hope to be at Ceylon and in Colombo under two weeks, whereas by air . . .

Already Mrs. Winter had selected an air agency and was dialling the phone.

'I wonder,' she said to Jane as she waited for a response, 'How long it takes to Colombo. 'Ah!' Into the receiver now. 'I didn't realize you were there. Only that much time, you say? Thank you so much. Now, will you give me departure details. Just twice a week! . . . Friday and Saturday? But that's days and days away.' It was Tuesday morning.

'Mother, it would take me that long to—' But even as she began to say it Jane realized that she could have left that morning. She had had all the necessary vaccinations. When April had made her overseas preparations, the injections had upset her so much that in the end, on her mother's suggestion, Jane had accompanied her and been injected, too. With a slight smile Jane now recalled that her own smallpox reaction had put April's to shame, nonetheless she had not regretted the precaution at that time, for – who knew? – she might need it sooner than she thought. And, as it was happening, she was needing it.

Or – the look at her mother's shocked face – was she? For her mother was delving now into fares.

'Three hundred and sixty dollars,' she echoed, 'a hundred and eighty pounds. 'You're sure that's the economy rate?'

Jane was squirming with embarrassment even though there was no one to witness her discomfort. When April had left Sydney even the best hadn't been good enough. The phone went down, and suddenly contrite, her mother assured her, 'I'm just thinking of you, darling, with your award plus all you can add to it, plus all I can spare, that terrible fare would still leave you very little to spend.'

Or to give to April?

Mrs. Winter, despite Jane's insistence that the rate would be the same wherever she applied, was now going through all the agencies in the pink pages. All at once unable to listen to the protests, Jane went out of the flat and down the stairs.

She remembered at the bottom step that she had not told Mr. Everett about the award ... nor what was to happen to her because of the award. That is, wryly, if Mother and the airline could come to terms. Even if they did not come to terms, and she remained here, Max Everett would still be interested in her success, then if they did, and a passage was booked, he must know at the earliest possible moment because he would have to look for a replacement for the position she had filled.

Mr. Everett 'arranged' things, parties, tours, projects, entertainments, lectures – the list was seemingly endless. Jane had spent three nights a week, from six to eleven, helping him with his accounts, all day Saturday. In this way she had been able to attend the Ackland Institute, and, because of the unusual thus better paid hours, her weekly pay envelopes had been as fat as if she had a daily nine-to-five job.

She found Mr. Everett busy on a pile of tickets. He was more often on tickets than anything else, so Jane, not so intrigued as she might have been had she not written up for him similar forms for faraway places, got straight into her news. Though before she could say much Max Everett got in first.

'Congratulations, Janey. I saw it in the paper. I suppose you're here now to tell me you won't be working for me any more.'

'I would be working for you if I wasn't going away. Two hundred dollars isn't a fortune.'

'Then,' interrupted Mr. Everett, 'why are you leaving work? Leaving me? No, don't tell me.' His smile was edged. 'April. Stranded somewhere. In need of our Jane.'

'Yes,' Jane said.

'Well, it's been nice knowing you, Janey, and heaven knows where I'll get a girl to toil the hours you did, but if you're going, you're going.'

Jane put in, '*If* I'm going,' and told him how much the award had been a second time and then the lowest fare to Colombo.

'Colombo? Ceylon?' He looked up with interest from his tickets. 'I'm working in that direction right now – a charter flight to Madras.' He looked down again and read: 'Sydney ... Darwin ... Singapore ... Madras. The usual Air-India route, though this time in a private craft instead of the company Boeing.'

'How many in the charter?' Jane's interest was instinctive; she had liked working on flights with Mr. Everett.

'It's a trade conference,' he told her, 'and the full load was to be fifty souls, but two drew out. I sold one of the seats at once to an outside ... out of the trade, that is ... and I reckoned at the rate I was getting from him that a complement of forty-nine travellers would be fair enough.' He started to smirk, then stopped suddenly to look, instead, at Jane. 'Or do I reckon that?' Now the satisfied smirk had grown into a speculative grin.

Jane grinned cheerfully back, not at all impressed. She knew these charters of Mr. Everett's, they were always run on strictly luxury lines, for which a passenger paid strictly luxury prices. No economy rates here – despite that contemplative expression on Max's face certainly no seat for her.

'You're wrong, Janey.' The agent had evidently read her thoughts. 'If I was satisfied with forty-nine for my party, it only stands to reason I'll be more satisfied still with forty-nine and a half. In other words you can have the seat for half fare.'

'Which is—?' asked Jane, still unenthusiastic, expecting from Max Everett as much plus a little more than the economy rate of a public craft.

Max said, 'A hundred and fifty. Will that do?'

'A hundred and fifty?'

'Yes.'

'Pounds, of course.'

'Dollars.'

'S–seventy-five pounds!' gasped Jane.

'You're right,' Jane.'

'But in the charters you arrange,' half-laughed, half-cried Jane, 'that's only a third fare.'

'In this instance it's actually a quarter, it's a real slap-up trip. But I reckon' – with a pat on Jane's shoulder — 'you're worth it.' He became busy again. 'How about health requirements? You'll only need smallpox from Australia, eight days after primary, up and to three years after secondary.'

'I've had that, and cholera and typhoid as well, with April.'

'Good girl! How long do you intend stopping? If it's under a month you won't need a visa.' At Jane's uncertain look, he added, 'You can always apply over there if you overstay your time, so that's no concern.'

Jane was glancing through his charter list to give herself time to collect her senses. She was feeling that everything was going much too fast for her. 'All of these tickets are for Madras,' she said, glad to find a hitch to halt the bewildering speed, 'If I went would I have to go to Madras first and then find my own way back to Colombo?'

'For a special girl I think we can arrange a special call.'

'When the special girl is only paying a special quarter fare?' asked Jane, still unsure.

'Why not? The other "outsider" is making up for you ... monetarily, I mean; I felt he could afford it.' Max Everett shrugged. 'After all, I got him included in a hurry so he must expect to pay for speed. Not that Senhor Camoes would ever argue over money ... he's too much the bland gentleman for that.'

'Senor? He's Spanish?' asked Jane.

'It's Sen-hor, Jane, and he's Portuguese.'

'That's a coincidence. I'm to fly to Colombo because April—' But Max Everett was not listening, he was busy including Jane on his list.

'You're not wasting any time,' Jane put in a little nervously.

'And you can't either. The charter leaves at noon.'

'What?' Jane was aghast.

'Noon. Still want that seat?'

'Of course ... though twelve o'clock is only a few hours away.'

'Three. While I'm making out your certificates, your entry endorsements, currency declarations, the rest, you better run home and pack your bags. No need to tell you about that.' He smiled, for it had been Jane's special job at the Agency to advise on what and what not to take.

As Jane still stood, he snapped his fingers under her nose. 'Everett for speed. Remember our slogan? Get going, girl, because I have a lot to do for our quarter fare.'

'Max ... Max, you're sure you're not losing over me?'

'All I'm losing is losing you. Don't be an idiot, Jane, it's the least I could do for the best secretary I've ever had. The charter leaves at one p.m., really, but you'll be required at Mascot an hour before that. Now scram, Janey, else I'll offer your fourth to Senhor Camoes, and probably he'd snap it up.'

'Is he that large to need it?' she laughed.

'Yes, he is large, as a matter of fact, but I was speaking more in the manner of exclusiveness, if this Portuguese gentleman could have chartered the entire craft I know he would have done so.'

'You mean he doesn't like people?'

'My dear Jane, I issue tickets, arrange flights, not delve into people's characters. Now, home with you, and back here at eleven. No, to make sure I'll come round to the flat, I'll drive you to Mascot myself.'

'You are a dear!' she smiled.

Max grinned again. 'Don't let my dear-ness go to your head,' he reminded in a mock-business manner as Jane hurried out of the office. 'You still have to part up that quarter fare.'

A quarter fare! Less than a child's fare! A luxury flight at that. It was, as the girls at Ackland would have said, 'a steal.'

19

As she scurried back to the flat Jane wondered briefly if she would keep some of the money facts of the trip to herself . . . she could tell her Mother that Max had offered her a reduced fare . . . she could say it was half, not a quarter, the usual rate . . . she could say . . .

But no, it was no use. The custom of sharing was so inherent in her that the moment she walked in she announced, 'It's all right, I can go.' Then to, dispel the dejected . . . and defeated, by the closed-up pink pages . . . look on her mother's face: 'Seventy-five pounds.'

'Seventy— Oh, darling. Oh, darling, darling wren!'

Darling *April*, deciphered Jane.

Together they packed, though Jane would have been quicker and more accurate, without her mother. Kindness, however prevented her from refusing the unsuitable cape that her mother pushed on her, embarrassment stopped her from pointing out that her travelling clothes were totally unsuitable for a luxury charter, that she should race into town and splurge some of the savings she had won on a sophisticated suit. She looked ruefully on her office-y navy linen with the almost schoolgirl white collar.

As though she read her thoughts her mother said anxiously, 'No one looks when you're travelling, darling and once you get to Colombo, then April can advise you. I've no doubt that there's lots of her things that she would be glad – I mean, you're both the same size.'

She really meant that April would be willing to pass over her present wardrobe and use Jane's money on a second issue, but she did not say it, of course, and Jane did not voice it. Of course.

A cup of tea . . . a last look round the flat that after all, was home, then Max Everett tooting impatiently at the front door, Jane reiterating to her mother that she needn't come to bid her farewell, her mother reiterating that she must see her brown wren away though really meaning that she must repeat right up to the last moment how Jane must be very circumspect, very *everything* that April desired, the two of them descended to the courtyard, got into the car, and were whisked off to Mascot.

Max talked for all of them all the way in, fortunately so, for Jane felt suddenly apprehensive and unsure of herself, and her mother was undoubtedly not with them but miles across the sea.

After Max had checked Jane's luggage for her, however, gone through all the details, put Jane and her mother in comfortable chairs to await their summons through the loudspeaker, he stopped talking and instead pressed Jane's hand. More than that he pressed, with a fatherly affection, his lips to Jane's cheek. Then he left before Jane could bid him goodbye. Dear Max Everett, she thought a little dewy-eyed. He had been a good boss.

'Gone!' said her mother astringently. 'I thought at least he would be taking me home.'

'He has a business,' Jane reminded her. 'Also we have a half hour's wait.'

'All the same—' complained Mrs. Winter. She decided not to pursue the grievance but to spend the half hour briefing Jane.

'Darling, you will remember how much this means to April? She never said so in actual words, but I do think this Rodriguez of hers must be quite – well, quite—'

Jane said for her, 'Rolling.'

'Jane!' A punitive pause. 'Not of course that money counts. I mean take Vernon, darling. Take – well, take Paul.'

'Did you know my father had no money when you married him?' asked Jane abruptly, and was shocked at the look in her mother's face. Or could she be shocked? she asked herself. A marriage so soon, so desperately soon, after real love.

'Jane!' her mother said again.

It was hard going after that. Mrs. Winter tried rather deflatedly to repeat April's cause, and at last Jane put the two of them out of their misery by pretending to hear her flight called.

Her mother knew she hadn't, but rose at once.

'This is it, then, darling. Give my paradise bird all of my— I mean give April my love. And – and Jane—'

'Yes, Mother, I'll do all I possibly can.' At least, thought Jane, I can afford Mother that.

'Thank you, darling. Goodbye little wren.' A flutter of a handkerchief at the terminal door and Mrs. Winter was gone.

Jane sat, aware of a great relief. It's terrible, she thought, but it's like a load off one's shoulders being rid of Mother. Fleetingly she wondered how she would feel if she were April and being farewelled by a parent who loved her with all her being, not just— not just—

But the thought was unbearable, and she turned away from it. Turned, literally, into the darkest eyes she had ever seen.

They were set in a smooth olive face, a face crowned with thick, shining, very black hair. That the owner, a man was extremely tall was evident in the length of the legs stretched from Jane's neighbouring chair almost twice as far as her own legs, had she stretched, not touched them, could have reached. For the rest, he was impeccably, if rather soberly and utterly formally, dressed. And he had a small, clipped moustache.

Undoubtedly this was all Jane might have gleaned of him as her glance flicked his had he not said at once, in a voice she could not quite put a finger to, so correct, so perfect it was: 'That was exceedingly neat. May I congratulate you? If the occasion arises I too must hear a summons in the air.'

She looked at him furiously at first, but quickly hiding

the anger in an innocent raise of her eyebrows. She *had*
hurried her mother off, thought her mother had been in
a hurry to go but it was none of this man's business and
the best way to tell him so was to appear uncompre-
hending.

She was unsuccessful. Even though she did not know
him she had the feeling that it would be very difficult to
evade an issue with him.

'Come,' he said a little impatiently, 'I am not reproach-
ing you, I am praising your skill.'

'What do you mean?' she queried distantly.

'Undoubtedly the position was becoming tedious.
How much more honest your handling of the situation
than the usual polite humbug that more often than not
takes over the controls. It was clever of you.' He made an
acknowledgment.

But Jane was annoyed. She was not pleased with herself over her dismissal of her mother, even though her
mother had rushed the opportunity to go. She was less
pleased that this man had edged himself into the act.

'I fail to see,' she said coldly 'what any of it has to
do with you.'

'You are right, of course but I was placed in this seat
by my representatives, and the Australian voice, I find is,
very clear.'

Australian voice. Then he was not Australian himself. Though, of course, that had been obvious from the
first. That perfect English, no short cuts no drawl or
slur.

Jane said tersely of her own Australian voice: 'Clear
– or loud?'

'I did not say loud,' he reproved.

There was a silence between them. Jane wondered if
she could get up and find another seat, but then her two
bags were at her feet, and if she did he would probably,
being the gentleman he undoubtedly was, rise to help

her, and she would feel more embarrassed again.

At that moment fortunately a noisy band of travellers arrived, by the affluent appearance of them probably Max Everett's trade bunch, and even if she had wanted to put the man in his place Jane doubted if she could have done so. The chatter drowned all the but official announcements; this time the Australian voice *was* loud.

Then:

'Flight 507, special charter to India,' was being intoned over the public address, 'please go to Gate Number Four,' and Jane rose as she had wanted to, first reaching for her bags.

But, as she had expected, the man beside her rose, too, took the bags for her.

'It's all right,' he answered as she protested, 'my own already have been attended to. I have empty hands.'

'But – but you can only take them as far as the barrier, and you'll lose this seat.' It was a busy departure hour, the terminal was packed.

'I do not need the seat,' he shrugged. 'I am leaving, too.'

'Then' – with a show of cordiality that she found rather hard but after all she would not see him any more – 'you must be leaving around the same time as I am.'

'That could be.'

They had reached the gate by now. An officer was examining Jane's ticket ... for a hysterical moment Jane wondered if it stated quarter-fare ... then the check-clerk was saying politely, 'thank you, madam. And' ... to the man bearing Jane's two bags ... 'thank you, sir.' They both passed through.

There was something wrong here. This was a chartered flight. They were all conference attendants, specialists in trade, only one outsider, except herself. Only one outsider, except— except—

But no, it couldn't be. And yet – and yet *Senhor* Camoes, Max had said.

She looked quickly and covertly at the man now striding beside her, noted the unfamiliar look. Portuguese? Quite feasibly. But, thank goodness, going to Madras in India, not Colombo in Ceylon. She was the only traveller for Colombo, so at least she had not put her foot into it, into April's ambitions, right from the start.

For, although he had commended her, spoken of her honesty and lack of humbug, Jane had had a feeling that the praise really had been damning, that for all his praise, as he had expressed it, that actually he had strongly disapproved.

Hower, Madras was India, and Colombo was Ceylon, and never the twain and all that. With luck this Rodriguez of April's, or at least Rodriguez's family, need never know that their new daughter's sister had not started off as far as they nationally were concerned in a suitable ... Portuguese ... manner.

The thing to do now was to avoid the man, sit as far from him as possible. Conversation, however hard one tried to be circumspect ... that favourite word of Mother's! ... often got into the wrong channels.

'May I sit—' began Jane to the bowing, sari-clad hostess who greeted her at the door.

'But yes, it has been arranged,' came the smiling answer before Jane could finish her request. 'The others, they are all of one mind.' The hostess gave a graceful gesture. 'They are all trade. After all, it is charter Flight. But you two most certainly can be spared details in which, naturally, you are not interested.' She was leading Jane down the passage.

Before Jane could protest, explain, before she could say a word, she was comfortably seated – Senhor Camoes seated by her side.

25

CHAPTER TWO

ALL the pre-departure things were being performed ...
the placing of the rest of the passengers, the adjustments
of head-rests, the fixing of seats and belts, the fastening
of doors. None of it took really long, and yet the silence
between Jane and the man now beside her seemed to
grow so abysmal that Jane wondered if the conversation could ever climb out of the depths.

But it did – by Senhor Camoes saying abruptly,
'Admitting that my presence is a surprise, and not a
pleasant one, it is still surely insufficient reason for dumb
dismay, senhorita.' He paused. 'I assume I am right in
that?'

'In the dumb dismay?' she managed to ask.

'The dumb dismay has been established. No, I refer
to senhorita. You are senhorita?'

Stiffly Jane said, 'I have no knowledge of Portuguese,
but if you ask am I miss, then I am.'

His lifted brows indicated that he would like her to
complete the self-presentation, but Jane left it at that.

He gave a slight shrug, said, 'I am Senhor Camoes,'
then, leaning forward deliberately to consult her neat
card, 'I am Joao Camoes, *Miss J. Winter*.'

'Jane,' complied Jane unwillingly, 'Miss Jane Winter.'

'So,' he said.

The engines were whirring. The plane was slowly
taxiing down the long runway. Ordinarily Jane, singu-
larly unused to travel for the average youthful Australian, would have been quivering with excitement, but
not this time, not with the probing black eyes of Senhor
Camoes on her.

'So sophisticated,' he remarked of Jane's studied calm.

'The young women of my country would have been in vapours of fears and pleasure.'

At that moment the craft left the ground, and in spite of her determination not to show any emotion in front of this man Jane thrilled at her first experience of wings.

'So,' he said once more, a little amused smile flicking the corners of his long sensitive mouth. He said nothing else, just that low, discerning, 'So.'

Jane was annoyed with herself that she felt obliged to offer explanations.

'I've never known anything like this,' she half-stammered. 'I've never flown before.'

'I can believe you have never flown previously, you are very young, senhorita, but not to know such things—' His quick gesture took in the obvious luxury of the expensive arrangements of the interior of the plane. He smiled a kindly reproof.

Jane understood at once. The very fact that she was on such a luxury flight made a travesty of her words. She began searching for a dampening response, one that would put him, and his deductions, in their right place, but he added before she could a formal, yet approving, 'It is well you are not experienced in travel, I think, for although I find the young spirit of your young country very commendable, I still believe in our own Portuguese safeguarding of those of the tender years.'

'Safeguarding or cloistering, senhor? And am I not a little beyond "tender years"?'

'If you were, senhorita, then undoubtedly it would be cloistering, but my eyes tell me that the bloom is still very much there.' He made a gallant inclination of his dark head.

A little embarrassed, for Australians did not pass such suave compliments and she was unused to them, Jane blurted, 'But you're very wrong, of course – if not in the age, then in the appearance. My name, senhor, may I remind you of my name?'

'Senhorita?'

'Jane.' She summoned up a wry smile for him.

'What is that, senhorita?' He looked puzzled.

'Plain Jane. Don't you have that in Portugal?'

'Plain Jane! You mean uncomely Jane? But you joke, of course. Or' – a searching glance – 'you are being coy?'

'I'm never coy.' That was true. With a sister like April it was no use trying tactics.

'Then I do not understand.' He shook his head.

'I am *plain*, senhor,' Jane said quite crossly. It was all right to admit indifference in looks in bright repartee, but not such fun to have to announce it in unadorned words. 'Thank you for the "bloom and tenderness",' she accepted drily, 'but it still doesn't alter an unassailable fact.'

'You must please yourself over that so-called fact,' he said a little carelessly, 'but I still award you bloom and youth.'

'Tenderness was also a word.'

'But not yours?' His brows raised quizzically. 'Yet tell me, senhorita, is there not a tenderness in you right now? Have you not left behind you, as all young women do, part of your heart?'

'I have left none of my heart. I and my heart are travelling together.'

'So,' he said.

The travellers were unbuckling their seat belts, forming their little groups. Each of them seemed to know someone else and the greetings were hearty.

'We are an island,' Senhor Camoes said softly.

The plane now had found its rhythm and its engines beat out the theme: the sari-clad hostesses moved like exotic butterflies in the rich Oriental decor.

The senhor was watching Jane, smiling slightly. 'Yes,' he said, still in the soft voice, 'in such a setting you are not Miss J. Winter but Maharanee.'

'And you a Majarajah.' She had caught the spirit.

'That calls for a royal toast.' He smiled at a soft-eyed attendant. 'A red wine for Miss Winter. I think perhaps' – he gave a name and vintage.

'And you, sir?'

'Since we are an island, we must take the same.'

'Sir?' The hostess's dark eyes were bewildered.

'We will both have the red wine.' There was an errant note of laughter in his voice, and though errantry was the last thing she would have believed in this smooth sophisticated man Jane found herself, too, concealing a smile.

'Our fellow travellers are relaxing,' pointed out the senhor presently, for the cigarette smoke now was weaving the groups together in a closer more hospitable circle. 'You, too, will have a cigarette, senhorita?'

'Thank you, no.' Something in his face as she refused made Jane ask, 'You seem disappointed, but surely you don't approve of smoking in the young and tender?'

'You are not one to forget,' he remarked mildly of her own remark. 'Yes, I am disappointed. Although I approve of the young and tender, as you put it—'

'No, *you* put **it**.'

'Not smoking,' he continued, ignoring her interruption, 'I must admit I am wishing to smoke myself.'

'Then do so by all means, Senhor Camoes.'

'You may not be so approving when you see my cheroot.'

'My employer smoked cigars, and that's what cheroots are, aren't they, and I loved the aroma.'

He had taken a case from his pocket, removed a long cigarillo from it and was clipping the end. 'Employer?' he half-frowned. Before she stumbled an explanation he said, 'But of course, you are Australian, and in Australia the girls do not sit at home and work fine lace.'

'Do they in Portugal?'

'In many places of Portugal.'

'Is – is that good?' Jane dared, and was relieved when he actually turned and smiled at her.

'I don't know,' he admitted. 'Perhaps I thought so once, but now I am not so sure.'

'This was your first trip to Australia?' she gathered ... but gathered wrongly.

'No. But' – a pull on the cheroot whose aroma Jane found quite as pleasurable as Max's cigars had been – 'this is the first time I have actually observed.'

'And why is that, senhor?'

'I have become interested. Very interested,' he returned.

'That sounds,' bantered Jane frivolously, 'like something to do with a woman.'

'It is,' he affirmed soberly.

The red wine arrived, but before it was poured the senhor tasted it critically.

'Yes, it will do.' He handed Jane the glass, took up a glass himself. 'Will our toast be,' he asked, 'to the young and tender? Or will it be to a whole-hearted traveller? Your words quite definitely this time, senhorita. You said: "I and my heart."'

'A whole-hearted traveller will do,' agreed Jane with a small shrug. She wasn't going to drink to the young and tender, she considered herself years beyond that.

Yet not so many years ... The throb of the engines, the contagious serenity of the composed and gracious hostesses, the lazy buzz of conversation, the blue drift of smoke and the aromatic air of the cheroot closed her eyes for her. She opened them with difficulty when the senhor made some remark, but her reply was hazy, unconnected. The lids closed again. The red wine loosened

her fingers, set her gently adrift. The last thing she heard
was the senhor intoning something in his soft formal voice.

The first thing she heard again was a teasing yet still
formal: 'So you are not young, my child. On one small
glass of wine you have slept four thousand kilometres.'

'Four thou—'

'We have arrived at Darwin, where we have twenty
minutes' stopover. Shall we walk around, look at the terminal displays?'

He asked her, but at the same time helped her to her
feet. A glance around her showed Jane that the plane already had emptied, so evidently it was expected that she
would alight.

She followed the senhor to the door and down the steps
to the airfield. It was still bright light, but of course
it would be. They had left Sydney early afternoon and
by air the Northern Territory capital was only four hours
away. All the same Jane felt a surprise. All those kilometres that the senhor had told her ... though she found
she could only think in miles ... and still the same daylight. She was glad, though, she had not expressed her
surprise. It would make her seem, to him, more the child
still.

But perhaps he sensed it in her, for, looking down on
the still sleep-dazed eyes, he promised with a hint of
amusement, 'Night will not catch up with us until we
are approaching Singapore. But do not be disheartened,
senhorita. By Madras I can promise you a big gold moon
and many silver stars.'

You needn't bother, Jane said to herself, for I won't
be seeing them, not in Madras.

It was too hot to leave the airport, and anyway, twenty
minutes was too short a time for any sightseeing, so Jane
simply looked at the souvenirs that departing travellers
could take with them if they wished ... and if they had
sufficient means. She had not.

31

She stroked the soft ears of a furry koala, but her eyes were on a flashing opal bracelet that Senhor Camoes was examining closely. Was he interested in it because of that 'interest' he had spoken about? 'Something,' she had interpreted boldly, 'to do with a woman?'

Evidently not – or so he presently implied. He explained, Jane still fondling the bear: 'I trade in gems.'

'Is that a good piece?' she asked.

'Excellent, though perhaps not as valuable as a black piece would be. The black opal is more popular, so, of course, its monetary value soars.'

'I prefer this.' Jane touched the deceptive pearly stones, deceptive because suddenly fire broke out from the gently gleaming depths, flashes of purple and gold.

'Yes,' he said, regarding her and the bracelet, 'the white opal would be for you, never the black.'

'Milk for a mouse.' Jane smiled faintly.

'Senhorita?'

'You would need more than Plain Jane to show off the black variety, senhor.'

'You are being coy again.'

'I said before, I'm never coy.'

'Yes, you said it,' he agreed blandly, and, annoyed, Jane put down the koala and went to examine some carved nulla-nullas.

Almost at once he joined her. 'Are you so angry with me,' he asked, 'That you take this revenge?' At her look of surprise he reminded her, 'The nulla-nulla was once a killing stick ... see, a Portuguese knows that Australian lore better than a native daughter ... and although I deserve reproof I think that the extreme action would be rather unfair. Especially' – putting the bear she had fondled into her arms – 'when I am a Portuguese bearing gifts.'

Mollified, Jane accepted the bear; she told herself that

32

at least she could do that. 'But you shouldn't,' she added banally.

He shrugged ... a frequent gesture of his, she had noted ... and the summons came to return to their plane.

They left Darwin ... and Australia ... and began winging their way through larkspur blue skies over larkspur blue water, a water that turned into a pale turquoise as they went farther and farther north. Once the plane flew lower to let the passengers see the dreamy, spicy islands that rose from the glassy seas, the trade ships that passed in almost endless procession: junks, sampans, some of the sampans with complete little houses built on them.

The sun set several hours before Singapore, set in a blazing triumph of crimson and gold.

'Soon,' said the senhor, 'you will have your moon and stars.'

Jane could not remember expressing a wish for moon and stars, only a secret satisfaction that the moon and stars she would see would be Sinhalese, not Indian. Not that she did not wish to include India in her experiences, but not in the company of this formal man. Even kindly as he undoubtedly was, as in all honesty she must admit he had been to her, he was still almost formidably formal, undoubtedly a force to be reckoned with. She had no wish to do any reckoning. She was going to have her hands full as it was. Full of April.

The triumph of crimson and gold gave way to eggshell pallor, then, in the way of the tropics, night came almost like the drop of a curtain.

'Instant evening,' the senhor smiled.

An exciting Indian meal was served, a curry very unlike the curries Jane had had at home, and so spiced and hot that but for the poppadoms that the senhor suggested she eat quite liberally with it perhaps a little too exotic for Jane's taste. But the delicious slices of tropical fruit helped, the cooling papaw and mango, and Jane at last put down the fork and sighed.

'That was lovely.'

'You like the new flavours, senhorita?'

'Very much.'

'Then that is good. You will enjoy India, too.'

Only I'm not going to India. I am getting off at the next exclusive ... exclusive for everyone but me ... stop. She should have told him this, it would not have hurt her, but for some reason she could not have explained Jane kept silent.

'You will be stopping in Madras only?' he asked.

'No.' That was true enough.

'Then that is good, too. To see India you must see more than the English metropolis.'

'English metropolis?'

'I exaggerate, of course, but Madras is more English than the other cities of India. Understandable, when you realize that it was founded by the English. Bombay was founded by my own people. Though they both are India, there is still, even after almost three centuries, a national difference.'

'Obviously you prefer your own Bombay,' deduced Jane.

'But I do not live there, senhorita,' he said rather in surprise.

Disconcerted ... and in some way vaguely uneasy ... Jane asked Senhor Camoes to tell her about Madras.

'To tell would be to spoil,' he smiled. 'I would not deprive you of the beauty that awaits you in Pantheon Road. It is a beautiful place, and only for the fact that it is not my place—'

His voice obviously halted for Jane's polite inquiry as to where was his place, where that is outside of Portugal, but she could not bring herself to do it.

'Then at least,' she suggested brightly, 'we can talk of Singapore.'

'Singapura, the Lion City, yes, indeed. It is a pity, senhorita, that again you will not have enough time to see it, though I promise you that the airport will be brighter than Darwin's, and that there will be more than a bracelet and a bear to buy.'

'But you didn't buy the bracelet,' Jane reminded him.

The Indian hostesses were coming around to help with seat belts, so there was no time for Senhor Camoes to reply. The plane put down.

Once outside the airport confines Jane could see what the senhor had meant when he had promised more brightness than at Darwin. It was a lush, tropical night, the sky fairly blazing with stars, and, the way it was in the tropics, shadows were more than dark here, they were indigo, they were deepest violet; light did not just gleam, it sprung out.

'It is a pity you could not have seen the Botanical Gardens, but at least you can look at the Malaysian dancers, hear some of the pedlars calling their wares,' the senhor said.

Jane watched a dance, marvelling at the delicate finger-work, refused lychee and sugar-cane juice from a drink pedlar and was glad that the summons to re-board the plane came before she succumbed to a shimmering jade green cheongsam that was being pressed on her at a quite ridiculous price. But ridiculous, or not, it was still money, and she did not know how long she might need her money. – Or April might need it. She turned at the summons and went back.

'You have a cool small head,' commended the senhor.

No, thought Jane, I have a slender purse. She hugged the bear to her, finding more pleasure in his soft fur than she believed she would have found in the satin moulding of the cheongsam.

35

The plane taxied off again. Coffee was served, little sweet cakes. The senhor insisted on more red wine, but this time Jane did not fall asleep after it. She gathered her things together instead.

'We have still some time to Madras,' the man beside her said lazily, his own eyes closed.

Jane did not reply. She did not know whether, as she had, he slipped off into sleep, but if he did he was certainly awake when the plane put down ... strictly briefly this time ... at Colombo.

The air hostesses were round Jane, making sure she had everything, and the senhor, opening his eyes, but not looking sleep-dazed as Jane had, so probably he had only been resting, said, 'But this is not Madras.'

'Colombo, sir.'

'We do not go to Colombo.'

'A special stop, sir. Not long enough, I regret, if you wished to shop.'

'I have no wish to shop. Good heavens, why would I when— But I did not know the trade conference was calling, too, at Ceylon.'

'Not the trade conference, sir.'

'Then—'

'The young lady.'

'There is only one young lady.'

Jane thought the rather unhappy hostesses had had enough. 'Yes,' she intervened calmly, 'I am the one.'

'You— But you are going to Madras.'

'I leave the plane at Colombo, Senhor Camoes.'

'You never said so.'

'I don't remember you asking.'

He went to reply, reply quite hotly, must have had second thoughts and closed his lips.

'You are being met, of course.' A full minute had gone by and all Jane's bags were accounted for.

'It is not,' said Jane, feeling her nerves so taut that

36

if she didn't speak out she would cry out, not caring if the hostesses heard or not, 'any business of yours.'

'But of course it's my business. It is – he looked at his watch – 'after nine o'clock. You saw for yourself how dark it was in Singapore, and that was barely nightfall. Now it will be pitch black. The tropics always are.'

'Presumably,' said Jane cuttingly, 'the city will be lit.'

'It pleases you to be flippant, senhorita, but it does not please me. I repeat ... and I would like to do more than repeat, I would like to question you closely, find out why you deceived me—'

'I did not deceive you, senhor, I simply kept my own business to myself.'

'All right, then.' His voice was testy. 'But I repeat, and I demand an answer, and I also feel so strongly about it that if you do not satisfy me with that answer I will leave the plane here also: *Are you being met?*'

'I,' said Jane meticulously, 'am being met.'

'Are you sure of that?'

'Quite sure.' Though even as she said it Jane knew she was *unsure*. Her mother as likely as not would have forgotten to cable. April, being April, would be late, or wouldn't turn up at all, or—

'Senhorita, I am coming to the terminal with you.' The senhor must have read her uncertainty.

'If you do the trade conference will complain that they were not told, either, of any stop at Colombo.'

He did not reply to that. He strode down the aisle to the steps that had been wheeled up, had a few brisk and to Jane indecipherable words to one of the pilots who had emerged from the controls, then preceded Jane to the tarmac, across the tarmac to the terminal.

'Your friend?' he asked shortly. 'You did not say which sex.'

Not a friend, a relation, female, a sister, a half-sister.

Jane could not have explained, but a quick searching glance had told her that April had done it again, done what she always did. She had not turned up. Perhaps she would come late. Or perhaps she would have forgotten altogether and Jane would have to make her own way. But one thing was certain ... and with flaming red hair like April's beautiful hair it was easy to be certain ... April was not there.

'Senhorita?' The senhor's cool but barely leashed voice reminded Jane that she had to do something, and do it quickly. Otherwise she would either be returned to the plane and taken on to Madras, or, and the prospect for some reason was worse still, the senhor would leave the plane with her.

'My friend,' said Jane flatly, 'has arrived. I thank you for your company. You've been most kind. I also' – clutching the koala tighter and finding a small reserve of courage in his touch – 'thank you for the bear.'

'But your friend, senhorita?'

'You won't have time to meet—' Jane glanced at the only European she could see – 'him.'

The Portuguese was looking, too. He appeared surprised. 'You mean—'

'Yes,' Jane said.

'In that case I shall not be meeting him.' If she had thought this man formal before, all Jane could have described was that then he had been indulging in high jinks. Bowing stiffly, he took Jane's hand and kissed it, but such a thin scornful kiss that it was more a derision than a salute, then, turning on his heel he strode away.

But only for a few steps. He paused, turned again, came back.

'You do not entirely satisfy me, senhorita.'

'Do I have to?'

'Yes. I would like to see you greet this friend.'

'By all means.' Jane's heart was sinking. None the less,

clutching the bear as though for courage, she walked across to the tall loose figure leaning indolently by the doorway, then, because the senhor was close on her heels and could hear if she spoke aloud, she rose to her toes and pressed her lips on a cheek she had never seen before, but not to salute him but to whisper, 'Please, *please*!'

She was uncomfortably aware of blue eyes too close to her for her peace of mind, tired eyes, slightly bloodshot, and just now impudently amused. But the man came up to scratch.

'Honey, I didn't see you. Forgive!' He kissed Jane back, and made no idle semblance of it. He kissed her again – on the lips.

'Senhorita Winter. Senhor Marsden.' It was the Portuguese speaking. He bowed. It was a derisive bow. Even Jane, unused to being bowed to at all, could not fail to see that.

Then the Senhor Camoes turned and went.

Vaguely Jane heard the whirr of the plane's engines ... she had come to recognize its sound now ... and she knew that the special Madras charter had started on its final leg. But what she could not realize was that she was here and not there, no longer in the comfortable, and comforting, lavish surroundings, that, in a few hours, had become a kind of home – a very delightful home.

Not that the terminal lacked the usual amenities, but, being a smaller port than Singapore, and being experienced at a later hour, there was an air of emptiness that rather worried Jane. She felt, as she had not felt previously, on foreign land.

Also there had been the company of Senhor Camoes, formal, it was true, yet just now Jane would have welcomed formality in place of the unashamedly bold blue eyes looking her up and down.

'Senhorita Winter, wasn't it?' The rather slack mouth twisted into a wry smile.

It was then that Jane remembered that the Portuguese had addressed this man, still leaning against the wall in the same indolent fashion as when she first had seen him, by name, too. Joao Camoes had acknowledged in a stiff, expressionless voice, 'Senhor Marsden,' and rather expressionlessly herself Jane now echoed the name he had intoned.

'Terry Marsden,' the man introduced himself.

He was looking at her in question, and seeing he had come to her rescue she supposed that at least she should return the courtesy.

'Jane Winter.'

'Countess? Duchess? Surely an Honourable at least?'

'Miss,' she told him.

'I didn't mean the matrimonial state.' He smiled – he had a rather fascinating smile even if it was faintly crooked. 'I meant the rank.'

'I'm Australian.'

'No, rank . . . oh, I see what you mean, you don't go in for titles Down Under, but you still could be Her Ladyship at least.'

'I'm not. You look surprised.'

He didn't really look it, obviously he was only pretending it, but she went along with him. 'Why are you surprised?' she asked.

'His Nibs,' Terry Marsden explained briefly. 'Senhor Camoes himself.'

'Well, what about him?'

'He isn't – isn't just Senhor. He's no less than a Count who prefers anonymity, but of course, that sort of thing gets around. My surprise was that he took upon himself a plain Miss.'

'He simply conducted me to the terminal,' said Jane rather crossly. She felt sure this Terry Marsden was teasing her, and she was not amused. A Count!

'Simple!' The man took her up on that. 'To avoid him you come to me, a perfect stranger, for help. Simplicity, my foot.' He was lighting a cigarette with nicotine-stained fingers that twitched slightly as he fumbled with the match.

'I can explain that,' she said haughtily, hoping the brushing-off attitude would discourage him.

But he said, 'I'm waiting.'

'Really—' she began, but he intervened.

'Yes, really, Miss Winter, you pick me up, you use me, then you expect me to accept being put down again at your convenience and not bleat back one word of Why? When? How come? Well' – exhaling – 'where will it be? In the coffee lounge here or in town in some hotel?' At a look in Jane's face, 'It has to be somewhere, girl, you're not going scot-free.'

It appeared by the April-empty terminal that she was not going anywhere, but Jane said, 'Here, then. I'm being met.'

He did not question that, but he did raise his brows. 'Bit late, isn't he?'

'It's my sister.' There was a sudden quiver to Jane's mouth, she felt all at once very lonely, quite bereft, and with an unexpected gentleness that was hard to believe in this brittle, tough man, Terry Marsden said, 'Sorry kid, she'll turn up. Meanwhile, we'll take a cup.'

He led her to a deserted lounge where he had to wake up an attendant and prod him into producing an indifferent brew.

'There's no craft expected in until early morning,' shrugged Terry Marsden of the coffee, and he took out another cigarette.

Considering the less than busyness, Jane wondered

what he was doing here. He must have anticipated the question she did not ask, for he drawled, 'I'm a journalist. I meet the planes.'

He was frowning as he said it, his fingers twitching again, and to tide over a rather awkward moment Jane asked, 'Do you represent the *Observer* by any chance?'

'I see you know something of us. By your bewildered look I should have thought you were new to the Pearl's bright shores.'

'Pearl's?' she queried.

'But Ceylon is the Pearl, surely you knew that? At least, it used to be, but now the tendency is to drop the last letter and call it the Pear.'

'You don't like it?'

'I have no feeling one way or other, it's just a place I happen to be in. But don't talk about me, you'll hear it all whether you're interested or not, talk about you. Why are you here?'

'I told you – I'm visiting my sister.'

'The one who hasn't turned up to meet you?'

'Yes.'

He frowned slightly. 'Can't say I've run into her.'

'I didn't think you would. She hasn't been in Colombo all that long.'

'Nonetheless I would have known; it's my job. But then she may be married?'

He meant, of course, that April's name might not be Winter. It was not, but Jane didn't bother to tell him so.

'She's not married,' she offered, 'and what do you mean that you should know because it's your job?'

'Just that. I meet the planes, write up the important people.'

'But April isn't—'

'You're going to say that your sister isn't a V.I.P., that she's the same as you.' My reply to that is that anyone who is personally conducted into a terminal by the Count

42

Joao Camoes, who has apparently travelled in the same craft, which undoubtedly would be a luxury aircraft, can't be anything else but a V.I.P. All right, young Jane, your turn.'

Jane sighed, but complied. It seemed she had to. Not only was the man persistent but the terminal was still April-empty.

'I'll tell you,' she said, and did, leaving out, of course. April's real reason for wanting her in Colombo in a hurry, that reason of impressing her family-to-be, or so April planned.

'Well, that's a bare bones story if I've heard one,' he accepted when she had done, and drained his cup. 'I think, Jane Winter, there's a few things you haven't told. However, I'll let you off, I'll even believe your incredible quarter fare story if you'll tell me why you need to put the Count off *that* much.'

'H-how much?' Jane blurted.

'As claiming me.' He lit up again. 'You couldn't have done a more damning thing had you struck him across the cheek.'

'I don't understand.'

'You will if you stop here long. Every city has its rake, its crook, its hard-time Harry. In this Pearl, or Pear, take you pick, I'm the one.'

'You mean,' interpreted Jane, 'you haven't the best of reputations?'

'Smart girl.' He nodded.

'But that couldn't affect Senhor Camoes,' said Jane, even as she protested remembering again ... and hollowly ... the Portuguese addressing Terry as Senhor Marsden. 'He's a resident of Madras.'

'Colombo.' Terry exhaled.

The Portuguese had said he did not live in Madras but he had known all about it ... he had been going there ... and she had disbelieved him.

'But I'm sure, 'she argued, 'that he . . . I mean the plane was bound for—'

'There would be a branch at Madras. Bombay, Calcutta, many more, no doubt. But the Camoes have always centred their activities in Ceylon.'

'I – I suppose there are many Portuguese here.' Let there be enough, anyway, to make it improbable, quite, quite remote, that Senhor Camoes knows April's Rodriguez

'I'll let you know the number.' Terry's voice was dry. 'Oh, yes, Sinhalese statistics is a branch of my newspaper duties, along with haunting the airport in the chance of an interesting character. Also classified ads.'

'It sounds interesting.'

'It's hell. I was a top grade journalist on the— But you don't want to hear that.'

Sympathetically she encouraged, 'I might.'

'You'd be sorry, and the sorrow wouldn't be for me but for yourself for listening. I told you about—'

'The rake, crook, hard-time Harry?'

'Yep. I brought it on myself. You know' – whimsically – 'I wouldn't tell everyone that, in fact I've never told anyone before, but you look, right now anyway, a lost sort of kid, as lost as Marsden himself.'

He ashed his cigarette and got up, took Jane up with him.

'But we'll find the lost girl, will we? What address?'

'It's here in my bag.' Jane fumbled in the bag's recesses and brought out April's letter. His dry 'Humph' rather disturbed her. 'Is it – is it—'

'A bad address? Heavens, no. Just a very average one. Bread and butter standard. Definitely no jam. Which proves, I suppose' – he flashed her a sudden and rather sweet smile – 'that your quarter fare story could be true. No sister to a genuine luxury passenger such as you appeared to be would stop at the Ranick. It's respectable and patronized by government servants, medium grade, no higher. Certainly no glamour.'

'Then it wouldn't suit April,' declared Jane.

'Only her purse, eh? Well, we'll find April.' He paid the attendant who was almost asleep again, then conducted Jane out of the terminal.

Many of the Sinhalese slept just where sleep had claimed them, in gutters, across footpaths, under dry, dusty trees. But many were still wide awake, even trading among themselves, and when they saw Jane they rushed at her, exhibiting their wares, mostly bean necklaces, wooden flutes, woven bags and the inevitable small black elephants.

They clamoured, they cajoled, they insisted, and Jane shuddered to think how she would have got on without the man at her side, now ridding her of her tormentors with a practised word here, a gesture there. She understood why Senhor Camoes had been so concerned at her arriving unaccompanied at a late hour on a private flight. With a routine arrival there would have been a small crowed to share the attentions of the pedlars, the airport would have had several guards on duty, porters and guides. Too late Jane regretted tossing back at the Portuguese when he had objected to her leaving the plane that unforgivable: 'It's not any business of yours.'

'Scram! Vamoose! Get cracking!' Terry Marsden was snapping his fingers as he said it. When he succeeded in forcing a path for Jane he snapped his fingers for a cab.

The driver, like the coffee bar man, was still half asleep, but a wave of a ten-rupee note under his nose took the dust from his eyes. He nodded without enthusiasm when Terry Marsden directed the Ranick, which made Jane think that Terry had been right, that it was not a glamour hotel, or, as the cab-man would be thinking, very promising for a large tip.

They drove through dark streets occasionally inter-spersed with bright markets, where, the same as at the airport, trade was being pursued over prone figures sleep-ing where sleep caught them.

'Why not?' said Terry. 'That's what sleep is for, strictly for sleeping. Ever slept under the stars?'

'Often, but it wasn't like this.'

'You mean you had a bag, a pump-up mattress, all the cons. But I'll bet you didn't have stars that size.'

'No,' agreed Jane, 'nor such a moon. Is it always per-fect weather like this?'

'There are monsoon periods, but the climate is always tropical. No woollens needed here, except in the Hills where it's much cooler, but I hardly think that someone who stops at the Ranick will be making a habit of that.'

'A habit?'

'Of going to the Hills for a cooler.'

'Is it exclusive?' asked Jane.

'Not as much as it was once, perhaps, but then none of Ceylon is.' He shrugged. 'Besides the Hills, the streams and coast now have a following, too.'

'But what do you mean, that none of Ceylon is the same as it was?'

'Just that. All the world over it's happening as it's happening here. The British ... or the French ... or what-have-you leave the country, and for a while a rot sets in. But from that rises a braver, more independent state. At least' – cynically – 'that's the idea. It's supposed to be just a matter of time.'

'You are British, Mr. Marsden?'

'Terry, Jane. Yes. There are a few of us still here.'

'As unhappy as you?'

'My unhappiness is Marsden, not Ceylon. No, I don't think they're unhappy. The place is looking a little tatty just now, but, like a small boy, it'll spruce up all right one day, and believe me, here there's some of the most glorious scenery in the world. Do you recall the beautiful background in that *River Kwai* film? In *Elephant Walk*? Then wait until you see the setting at Mount Lavinia – creamy surf, coconut trees, just everyone's dream of a tropical paradise come true. No, there's no reason to be . like Marsden. Ah, here we are at the Ranick now.'

Jane peered out and saw an indifferent building, all the more indifferent because of the flamboyant setting, a circle of wind-ruffled palms with stars caught in their branches. One had spiked the full gold moon.

But the hotel was not flamboyant, it was distinctly dull. The man beside her must have read Jane's thoughts, for he assured her, 'It's quite all right really, as I said, it's just strictly non-glamour and making no bones about that fact. If your sister's in the same quarter fare category as you affirm you are what else did you expect?'

'April has a Ritz taste,' admitted Jane. 'It's hard to see her here.'

'*Is* she here?' he asked.

'It says so in her letter.'

'Well, that's the right letterhead,' he conceded, glancing at the piece of paper that Jane held aloft. 'I'll go and ask at the desk.'

He was gone before Jane could tell him to ask for Winthrop, not Winter. She bit her lip.

When he returned his face was a study.

'Look, Jane, she's never even signed in, no Winter at all.'

'I know,' said Jane, ashamed now that she had not confided more in this helpful man, rake, crook, hard-time Harry though he might be. 'Her name is Winthrop. We're half-sisters.'

A light had come into his eyes, to Jane it looked like recognition, but all he said was a reproachful, 'You might have told me.'

47

'I might,' she agreed humbly, and got out of the car and walked up the steps to the vestibule herself.

But when the clerk, questioned, gave his answer, she was glad that Terry Marsden had come up behind her. When the Sinhalese behind the desk said in perfect English: 'Miss Winthrop has left, she has gone to the Shangri-la, gone this afternoon,' Jane was glad to have Terry to turn to, to lean on once more.

April, she thought, doing the same old thing, even in Ceylon. April, never reliable, never where you expected her. Where was this Shangri-la? What sort of place? Why had she left the Ranick Hotel?

When – if – they traced her at the new hostelry, if hostelry it was, what then?

CHAPTER THREE

TERRY had led Jane back to the taxi ... and that was another thing. Taxis cost money, Jane had no idea as to how much they cost in Ceylon, and the little money that Jane had might be needed for a long time.

Putting nicotine-stained fingers lightly on hers, Terry said, 'Not to worry, the bill's on me.'

'That is a worry.'

'All right, Miss Independence, on my expense account then, if I word you as an important person we'll get this taxi free.'

She gave a rather wobbly smile, then, still disturbed by that recognition, or she had thought it recognition, in his face when she had corrected, 'Winthrop', she asked, 'You've met April, haven't you, Terry?'

'I've seen her,' he agreed. As her eyes clouded in worry, he assured her, 'That's why I get a weekly pay packet, goose, to see people — it's my job, and teeming though Colombo is with Sinhalese, Moors and Malays, the proportion of Europeans is not so large that I could fail to notice one flame-haired, turquoise-eyed girl.'

'Undoubtedly,' said Jane of his description, 'that is April.'

When they had returned to the taxi, Terry had instructed the driver to the Shangri-la, and much more cheerful now, probably with a very large tip in view instead of the mediocre one associated with the Ranick, the Sinhalese began threading his way through the city, each turn of the wheels taking them through a more favoured area of Colombo.

'As you must perceive,' drawled Terry Marsden laconically, 'your sister's second choice of an hotel is in a

49

very different end of town.' His glance at Jane, had she noticed it, was narrowed, speculative.

But Jane did not notice. She was nagged with possibilities and probabilities to do with her half-sister.

'Why did April move?' she fretted to herself, but in her concern still loud enough for Marsden to hear. 'If this is a better hotel, as it seems it might be by the better neighbourhood, where did she get the money?'

'It is,' interrupted the journalist quite flatly, 'not just a better hotel but a luxury hotel. 'No, take that back. It's a *super* luxury abode.'

'But – but––'

'Exactly,' he agreed significantly.

His eyes were narrowed again on Jane, the cynical twist back on his lips. He seemed sourly amused at his own thoughts, but – after a long, long look at the girl beside him – he did not express those thoughts.

'Where did you see April?' Jane asked him.

'I cover the ships, too. Your sister, if I remember rightly, came in the *Fairhaven*.'

'Yes. She was to go right through to Southampton. I can't think why she disembarked here.'

'Can't you?' Another look, then an abrupt softening in the hard face. 'Young love and all that,' Terry lightly suggested.

'You mean, of course, this Rodriguez?'

'Oh, so you do know about it.' Once more the tight estimation.

'Just – just that she's fallen in love. No details of where they met, when they met. Nothing at all, really, not even his name, or connections, not anything.'

'Ah.' It was only a half breath really from Terry Marsden. He looked faintly amused.

'They would meet,' he informed Jane, 'when Miss Winthrop came ashore with the rest of the tourists to see Colombo.'

'But surely the ship wouldn't stop long enough for – for—'

'For two people to fall in love?'

'For April to make such a big decision as to leave her ship less than half way through the trip.'

'It depends,' said Terry Marsden drily, 'on the prospects.'

'What do you mean?' Jane's acorn eyes that matched her hair exactly were wide and troubled.

'Prospects, Jane. Hasn't love many prospects?' He made it a laughing evasion.

She smiled with him, and he asked a little cagily, 'But where do you come in? I mean why have you flown over? Not even come leisurely by ship? No, don't tell me, it's to impress the family, isn't it? You've come on a sisterly crusade, and why not? You've got just that sweet, impressing look that would win a mission, you're not at all like April.'

'That could be. We're only half-sisters. April is our paradise bird. I'm the brown wren.'

'In England we think highly of our brown wrens.'

'Well,' said Jane with an earnestness there was no mistaking, 'I trust the Portuguese will think highly of me.'

'And through you your sister?'

'Yes.' A little challengingly, 'Is there anything wrong in that?'

'No,' said Terry Marsden. But he added to himself, 'Except that you've made a very unfortunate start.'

The taxi was coming to a halt, and already the driver was arguing over the fare.

'Take no notice,' advised Terry, 'It's always like this. Finally we come to a mutual agreement.'

But Jane was barely listening. She was looking ... a little aghast ... at the Shangri-la. If the Ranick had set her back with its air of respectable seediness the

51

Shangri-la set her much further back with its grandeur. Why – why, the place was literally a palace.

Imposingly large, blazing white, lavishly flanked by tropical palms and Temple trees, which were necklaced, now it was night, by strings of coloured lights, fountains playing in paved courts, an orchestra stringing a dulcet tune, dark waiters in long robes with green cummer-bunds and with sandals on their feet, a truly remarkable red carpet on which to enter, the Shangri-la had the effect on Jane of making her want to shrink back into the car.

'Oh, come!' grinned Terry crookedly. 'Your sister would walk down like the duchess I believed you were.'

'How would you know?' asked Jane. 'You haven't met her.'

'I told you I'd seen her, and I must now add to that statement, for I must have met her, mustn't I, to have introduced her to Rod.'

'Rod?'

'Rodriguez.'

'You – you introduced her to this man?'

'Yes.'

'But how? I mean you two hadn't previously met—'

'That's easy.' His voice was laconic. 'She asked me to.'

'She—' But Jane did not go on. Flushing with embarrassment, she saw in her mind what she had seen with her eyes many, many times – April using people. April riding roughshod over people to get what she wanted. April, seeing this Rodriguez no doubt getting out of a lavish car, for it would take more than good looks to attract April, turning to the journalist who had met the tender from the *Fairhaven* to write up any important people and demanding, for April always demanded, to be presented.

'I'm sorry,' Jane said impulsively.

'For what?' She was pleased. He, undoubtedly, was pleased.'

'And you?'

'I was amused.'

'Amused?' she echoed.

'At the thought of her stricken look, after the presentation, when Rod would tell her, as undoubtedly he must tell her, being a true Portuguese and always solicitous towards the fairer sex, that her presenter was a rake, a crook—'

Jane murmured, 'A hard-time Harry. But you're not, are you? You're – you're kind.'

He looked at her with a soberness she had not seen in him before. 'Thank you, Jane,' he said. 'And now shoulders back, head up. You may not be a duchess officially, but you are – to me.' He pressed her arm and together they went down the fabulous red carpet.

Halfway to the reception desk an imposing figure in tropical hotel uniform hurried across to them.

'Madame? Sir?' A deep bow.

'Miss Winthrop,' said Terry, and Jane held her breath. If April had gone on from here . . .

But of course April hadn't. She might have known that April could not tear herself from such luxury.

'Certainly, madame, sir. The Rainbow Suite on the third floor.'

Oh, no! groaned Jane inwardly. Oh, no, not a suite!

Terry's fingers were under her arm again, quite firm this time, affording her strength. To the hotel official's 'Shall I call Miss Winthrop?' he answered casually, 'Don't bother, we'll go up.'

But at that moment Jane saw that it would be of no avail to go up, because April was not in her suite, she was sitting, alone, in a corner seat of one of the lavish lounges – the Kismet Lounge, Jane read in gold lettering, and, ostensibly, she was listening intently to the orchestra. But Jane, knowing April, knew that she was only listening to her own thoughts, that any attention left over from that was on her physical self, what effect she was having on the other loungers, whether any of them would be worth the fanning of those quite fabulous lashes over those perfect coral-washed cheeks, the pretty pushing-back movement she practised on her flame-red hair.

Still, that was April, and for all her infuriating though enchanting gestures she was still Jane's half-sister, the family's paradise bird. I suppose, thought Jane, despairingly, I love her, I must do to let her worry me like she does.

Terry had seen her, too ... how could he fail to miss her loveliness, all the more spectacular now in a shimmering lamé suit of red-gold to match her hair? That suit! Jane had never seen it before. April must have been buying up, and ... apprehensively ... buying up if not big, or so Jane hoped, then certainly ambitiously. That ensemble would have cost the world. April did not have the world, nor anything like it.

'Come along,' said Terry.

They walked along another red carpet to the Kismet, Jane said, 'April,' and her half-sister looked up.

She made a charming little moue of shame when she saw Jane, began an apologetic 'Darling, I completely forgot—' then her glance fell on Terry.

'You,' she said.

He wasted no time on argument or reprisal, he just said briefly, 'I'll have your bags sent up, Kid,' to Jane, flicked April a long derisive look, bowed to them both and went.

'That man!' fumed April. To Jane she said, 'Sit down, for goodness' sake. You look terribly travelled.'

'I am,' reminded Jane.

'Well, I said I was sorry. Jane, sit down, people are looking.'

Tired, knowing she was showing the signs of her journey, Jane said, 'Isn't that what you want?' but still obeyed.

April flicked a signal to a waiter in that experienced way of hers, then turned to her sister.

'Really, Jane, how could you embarrass me by arriving with *him*!'

'You mean—' said Jane deliberately, 'that he's a rake, a crook, a—'

'Here, in Colombo, he is not thought well of,' said April haughtily, 'and being in the position that I am I think it's very unkind of you to make a show of me like this.'

'In what position are you?' asked Jane carefully.

'You know very well. That's why you're here. I'm practically married into the richest family in all India and Ceylon.'

'Don't you think,' asked Jane, 'if it's still not quite clinched' . . . April shuddered delicately . . . 'that you're rather foolish sitting here unescorted in a hotel lounge? Keeping in mind, I mean, that the Portuguese are careful about such things.'

April's turquoise eyes indicated triumphantly that she would not have been unescorted very long, but to Jane she tossed, 'Roddy wouldn't care. He adores café society like I do, he's a pet, Jane, I really do love him to distraction, it's not just the prospects.' For a moment her turquoise eyes looked purely into Jane's acorn . . .

Jane, rather touched, leaned across and squeezed her hand. 'I'm glad of that. But if Rodriguez is so open-minded why are you angry that Terry Marsden came to my rescue tonight? Especially' – taking her hand away – 'when he came to *your* rescue when you wanted to meet this Rodriguez of yours.'

April pouted her full red lips. 'Terry Marsden is just one of those people who isn't done. You know what I mean. Roddy doesn't particularly object to him, but he did tell me after we had been introduced and Marsden had left us that he was not widely accepted, and most certainly not accepted by his own family, nor, and most important of all, by his uncle.'

'Have you met this important uncle, April?'

'He's out of Colombo just now. Roddy seems a little uncertain of him, but I'm not. You know I've always been with old uncles and things. She gave a gay little laugh. She sobered at once, though. 'But all the same I don't want to start on the wrong foot, and you coming in with that person is the wrong foot.'

'Then I'm sorry,' said Jane, 'but I still think it was preferable to waiting in the airport all night.'

'Darling, you could have found your own way.'

'To the Ranick?' Jane's eyes reproved April.

'That place was dreary. Roddy agreed with me when I said I simply must move. I was a little let down when he didn't . . . when he . . .'

Jane thought she knew what April was *not* saying.

'Where are you getting the money for a suite in this hotel?' she asked at once.

'Why, darling, not from Roddy, of course. Not from anybody. I mean in a position such as I'm in now I must be very circumspect.' Circumspect – Mother's little word.

Jane looked at her half-sister shrewdly. She could see that she was disappointed that Rodriguez had not pre-settled the bill. But Jane instead was relieved. Even though April would lightly dismiss it as a loan, it was still something that must not be done, especially, as April had pointed out, in her position.

But if Rodriguez was not paying it, nor anybody else, who was?

'April, have you been singing on the ship? Earning money?'

'In that luxury suite? I would have looked a fool. No, I just signed in here and they took me gladly. After all, just to be accompanied by Roddy is enough. And then you must admit I don't appear as poor as I am.' Again a gay laugh.

'Not in those clothes, anyway. April, are they—'

'Darling, nobody pays cash these days. Please don't fuss. Look upon them as an investment, the biggest investment I've ever made. Roddy's family, which really stops, apart from distant relatives, at the uncle, and thank heaven, for I'd loathe a lot of encumbrances like brothers, sisters and aunts, is quite tremendously rich. They're agents, only Roddy says that's really a misnomer because they own and don't just represent, and Jane, the things they deal in! Not just tea and coffee, rubber, coconut, mahogany and satinwood, but' – her turquoise eyes glowed – 'jewels. Roddy told me about the sapphires. Then rubies, Jane – the sought-after pigeon's blood.'

'April,' interrupted Jane anxiously, 'you did say you really liked Rodriguez?'

'Oh, yes.' April did not hesitate. 'I love him, Jane. I'll not deny that I was attracted by what he has. After all ... But he's very sweet, and we took to each other at once.'

It was not the ideal basis, but, for April, it was as substantial as one could hope. And the good thing was that in the beginning April had been attracted by the young man himself, plus car perhaps, and chauffeur, but not by the sapphires and rubies. They had come later.

'When we go upstairs we must delve into the money problem,' Jane frowned. 'I don't like taking crdit like this.'

'It's an investment, as I said, but I do think a money conference is a good thing. We'll go at once. How much have you brought?'

'Not much—' began Jane, then she asked, worriedly, 'Where am I to sleep?'

'Here, silly. I booked for you as well, hence the suite.'
April got up her graceful way and preceded Jane out of
the lounge to the lift. At the third floor they traversed
more red carpet to a satinwood door. April opened it,
and this time let Jane go ahead.

It was what Jane would have expected of April, large,
lavish and reeking of extravagance. She stifled a sigh.

April threw herself down on the bed and laughed,
'How much is not much, darling? Break the bad news.'

'It is bad.' Jane told her.

But April was not so concerned as Jane had thought.
'I hoped for more, but I didn't really think there would
be. Poor Mummy, if you can't win in two attempts what
hope have you? I mean, Jane, for your father to be poor
as well as mine! For us both be left only a pittance!' Jane
forebore to remind April that only she, Jane, had been
left anything, even though it hadn't turned out like that.
'One thing' – April resumed narrowly— 'that won't
happen to me.' At the look in her half-sister's face she
reassured her, 'But I do like him, I like Roddy tremendously, and you will, too. You will want to do what I
want you to, Jane, help me impress this uncle so that he
gives his blessing. It must be a Portuguese tradition that
the relatives wholeheartedly approve. So far as I'm concerned, I'd snap my fingers, but Roddy says it's important we do the right thing. And I suppose it is, too,
for after we're married we intend leaving Ceylon ... it's
fun for a while, but frightfully limited.'

'with all those shrines to visit, those plantations,
those—'

'I mean society, silly. It's the same old set. Roddy says
that Monelva, fairly near their old family home, is really
smart, then, of course, everyone knows that Lisbon is
international. We'd like to go amicably, so there won't be
any finger-snapping, just April looking demure and
presenting a sister in whose mouth most assuredly butter

would not melt. Darling Jane, thank you for being what you are.'

'Dull?'

April took off her gold suit and while Jane hung it up said magnaminously, 'I forgive you for turning up with that Marsden man, anyway. I don't think many noticed.'

'No, they would be looking at you.'

'Yes,' accepted April quite calmly. 'But don't do it again. I mean it's bad enough to start off on the wrong foot, but it would be catastrophic to continue the mistake.'

After she had snapped out her bed light Jane remembered, on leaving Sydney, thinking rather in the same strain. She had not wanted to start off in an unsuitable ... Portuguese unsuitable ... manner. The fear had come, she recalled, when she had discovered that the man who had been walking beside her to the plane was Portuguese. At the moment it had seemed just too much of a coincidence, only, fortunately, he had been going to Madras, not Colombo.

Then at once, and rather hollowly, she was recalling Terry Marsden remarking that the Camoes had branches also in India, at Bombay, Calcutta, other places, but that the centre was in Ceylon. She remembered asking him if there were many Portuguese in the island ... remembered Terry forgetting to tell her.

A cold finger touched Jane.

'April!' she called.

No answer.

'*April*.'

'Oh, really, Jane!' April came reluctantly out of her first light sleep.

'Your Roddy — what's his name?'

'Rodriguez, of course.'

'But his next name — his surname?'

April giggled a little. 'I can't pronounce it properly

yet – isn't that mad? I'm going to marry him and I can't pronounce his name.'

'What is it?'

'Carreras. I'll be the Senhora Carreras and I'll live in this beautiful home in this *avenida* that Roddy has told me about. Jane, are you asleep?'

Jane was not, but she felt she would be asleep quite soon. It had been a long day, a tiring day, and tomorrow was tomorrow and not to be dealt with until then. Especially when April's Roddy was Rodriguez Carreras, not Camoes as she had feared.

Jane felt her limbs slacken.

She wakened in the same cheerful spirit, wakened to iced lime juice, slivered papaw, a jug of coffee, cream, a rack of crisp toast. There was a small dish of marmalade and a curl of butter, all served on a silver tray. It was rather nice to be treated as though you were rich, Jane thought.

April came in from her bath, even more beautiful without her careful make-up. She sat on Jane's bed and buttered a piece of her toast and ate it. 'If you're hungry I'll ring for more.'

'Where's you own?' Jane was rather hungry.

'I'm breakfasting on the terrace, with Roddy. I'll bring you along next time, darling, but this morning – well, I haven't seen Roddy for two days, he's been in Madras.'

Madras.

However, Jane was determined not to cloud her new cheerful spirit. She smiled at April, said something foolish about young love, and when April directed her to come just at the end of the meal to meet Roddy . . . 'looksweet and serene and every inch the lady, Jane' . . . she agreed.

April went through Jane's clothes, snorting her disgust.

'Mummy shouldn't have let you come like this!' she exclaimed.

It was, thought Jane, actually the first time April had mentioned their mother.

'I'll find you something of mine. No need to panic, it will be one of the articles I brought from Sydney, so at least it will be paid for.' April heaved a sigh and said, 'I'm glad I don't limp through life.'

'If limping means paying one's way—'

'Oh, Jane, spare me. This is going to be quite a day, I'll need all my resources. Roddy will have seen his uncle, no doubt have something to report. Don't needle me before I start.'

'If loving Rodriguez is going to affect you like this,' demurred Jane, 'I think you should do some serious considering, April.'

'I've considered,' assured April, 'and don't worry, once I'm Senhora Carreras someone else will do the worrying. And I' – she smiled wickedly – 'the needling. This doddering, dependent old uncle, for instance—'

'How do you know he is dependent?'

'If not exactly on Rod's money, I mean if he has a little money of his own, then assuredly he is dependent on Rod's youth. Firms are always like that. The young carry the old.' April pulled a bright orange sheath over her head, a tangerine that should have clashed with her hair, but, because it was April, became part of her.

As Jane watched her, her own bright spirits diminished. April was too young and too lovely to be so coolly calculating. She felt too young herself, if not lovely, to be a party to such connivance.

'April, I don't like it,' she said.

April, about to toss something astringent at her, changed her mind ... and changed Jane's with her next words.

'Just waitt till you see Roddy, Jane, see him – with me.' Her turquoise eyes appealed, and when April appealed . . .

'All right,' Jane agreed.

After her half-sister had gone in a mist of fresh morning fragrance . . . April was very clever with her perfumes . . . Jane got up and went to the window. In the starlight and moonlight of last night she had only received a hazy impression of the part of Ceylon, of the dropped pearl to which she had come, so now she looked out with curiosity. With a little dismay. Yet withal an extent of thrall.

The dismay was because of the seediness . . . the same as she had sensed last night . . . making a pear of the pearl, and not a very appetising pear at that. For beyond the lavish grounds of the Shangri-la a different story unfolded, the story of a too-sharply divided economy, told, once beyond the hotel's handsome gates, in teeming crowds and clamouring, scantily-clad children. But the thrall was in the bare bones of the picture, if you could overlook the seediness, in graceful palm and Temple tree, in the distant glimpse of a Buddha in meditation, of a sky so blue that it seemed part of a postcard and not existing in fact at all.

A rickshaw went by, a very small coffee-coloured boy in tiny pants but carrying a huge umbrella, an oxen waggon, a girl with a red oleander in her black hair.

The same articles of trade with which she had been pestered last night at the airport were being clamoured . . . Jane wondered that any business was transacted, for surely everyone in Ceylon already had a bean necklace, a wooden flute, a small black elephant. Drinks were being peddled . . . probably lychee juice, sugar-cane juice. Little portions of dried seasoned fish were becoming even drier in the blazing sun as they waited to be consumed by some hungry customer.

Laughing a little, Jane withdrew from the window, then saw, rather to her dismay, for April liked her plans to go off like clockwork, that she had delayed longer than she should. She hurried into the pale green, button-up linen that her half-sister had allotted her, buckled sandals on her bare feet, ran a comb through the soft, straight, acorn hair and hurried out to the lift.

She found her way to the breakfast terrace and was relieved to see that she was in time. Indeed, by April's gay signal, she had timed it well, the pair, Rodriguez and her sister, had finished the meal and were sipping coffee.

But as Jane came nearer to the table beneath the striped umbrella April did not look so gay. Her eyes now were on the apple green linen she had given away, and they were sulky.

Rodriguez, as Jane approached, had got smartly to his feet to bow gallantly. He insisted that Jane take his seat while he called for another chair. When one did not come he murmured a word of apology and hurried off to question the delay.

'That green,' said April, 'doesn't suit you, you're too brown, Jane.'

'Yes, a brown wren. We can't all be paradise birds.'

That mollified April slightly. A look in her handbag mirror mollified her a great deal more.

'What do you think of him?' she asked.

'We haven't met yet.'

'Yes, but what do you think?'

'He looks very nice.' He had looked very nice – young, straight, faintly olive-skinned, smiling-eyed, boyishly fresh and clean. Nice.

'There was nothing much to report,' reported April, 'except that the uncle is returning to Colombo today. We'll meet him, Jane. You'll do your gentle refined act.'

'And you?'

'What I would like to do would be to put him in his place. I must admit that Roddy's deference rather maddens me. Anyone would think ... However, Roddy persists in being respectful, so I suppose it's an old Portuguese custom. But I can tell you, Jane, that once I'm Senhora Carreras – Here's Roddy now.'

Behind Rodriguez Carreras came a steward with a chair. The young Portuguese sat down, ordered more coffee, for three this time, replied to Jane's protest a laughing, 'But no, sister of April, at least if you will not eat with us you will drink with us,' then turned to April for introductions.

'Jane.' His hand was in Jane's, warm, sincere, a good friendly grip. Yes, he is nice, thought Jane again.

They talked busily together about many things, but when the conversation centred on Ceylon topics, the country's national and religious festivals, their cottage industries, April became bored. She sat it out until Jane asked Rodriguez about the ruined cities, a subject that always had intrigued her.

'My uncle knows much more than I do. You must get him to tell you of Anuradhapura, the ancient capital.'

'Of course he would know more, Roddy,' pouted April. He's older.'

'But not two and a half thousand years older,' said Rodriguez with delight. 'You are a dear, mad girl!'

April gave a pretty moue, asked to be excused to comb her hair and ran off. Rodriguez watched her go with unconcealed adoration. He *is* in love, Jane thought. But when he turned again to Jane the delighted amusement had given way to a small frown of concern.

'Your sister seems to think that my uncle is Methuselah,' he profferred troublously.

'When one is twenty-two, anything over that does seem rather old.'

'But you are younger than April.'

'Not much.'

'Yet you do not think like that?'

Jane got over the hurdle by smiling, 'Is it that important?'

'Not at all, but – but something else is. It's April's attitude to my uncle. Jane – I may call you Jane? – I have a feeling that April doesn't realize, appreciate, understand that—'

Jane understood without Rodriguez explaining any further. Obviously he was worried by April's carefree, one could say careless, attitude to people. To be concise, to Rodriguez's uncle.

'I think you're making a mountain out of a molehill,' she smiled encouragingly. 'I wouldn't worry, such an attitude *is* April. She doesn't really mean it, of course. She's thistledown, Rodriguez . . . do you have those in your native Monelva?'

His face had brightened again. 'So April told you!'

'Yes. And of the beautiful home in the *avenida*.'

'But the home,' said Rodriguez, 'is just that, it is not like my uncle's. I mean—' He stopped. April was returning to the table, and the morning sun was catching the pure flame-gold of her hair.

'She is so lovely,' he said almost painfully.

'Yes. A paradise bird.'

They lingered over their coffee, for Rodriguez said there was no hurry to go out to the airport to meet the plane. He commended April on having such a sister as Jane. 'My uncle will be favourably impressed,' he smiled. 'It is a splendid idea to have a member of the family present, and such a member.' He bowed. 'My uncle,' he explained, 'is very Portuguese in his views. I am, too, I suppose, but being junior—'

'Not junior, darling, just young.' It was April – pouting, not liking Rodriguez to be a junior in his firm.

'When he comes into the terminal,' continued Rodriguez, 'and sees Jane—'

'But I'm not going out to the airport.' The airport was the last place that Jane did want to go to. Her memories of last night were too recent – and painful. She heard again that frigid: 'Senhorita Winter. Senhor Marsden.' She saw the tall, straight back of Joao Camoes returning to the Madras-bound plane.

'But of course you're coming!' It was April and Rodriguez together.

The Portuguese said. 'It is most important, Jane, that April has a companion. It is also important, and you must forgive me, that the companion is not like her sister. I mean – well—'

'Roddy means that the companion is essentially a lady.' April's turquoise eyes laughed at the young man and their glances merged.

Feeling distinctly a third, and very uncomfortable, and *still* anxious not to go, Jane offered to meet the gentleman in question at the hotel.

'It won't do,' refused Rodriguez.

'You promised,' declared April.

With a sigh Jane complied.

As the plane was not scheduled until noon, the three of them wandered out to the paved courtyard where they sat for a while near the playing fountain, then on Jane's request they went to the nearby fish-pond to observe the beautiful tropical specimens that Ceylon had to offer, then later on Rodriquez's suggestion to the datura tree, just now in full bloom.

While Jane was delighting in the convolvulous-like blossoms . . . snowy-white at morning, related Rodriguez, but turning pink and purple as they faded at the end of the day . . . April decided it was time she changed her dress for her meeting with Roddy's uncle.

'But you look so beautiful,' he pleaded.

'And unsuitable?' she teased. 'No, darling, I intend wearing a silk suit.' – Silk suit! Jane flinched. There had been no silk suit in April's original wardrobe.

'Also, when I get back, Jane must change.' April's eyes on her sister were suddenly narrowed.

'But surely Jane is very suitable,' protested Rodriguez. 'That spring green is definitely Jane.'

That was the trouble. It was. April said flatly, 'I'll lay something out. Oh, yes' – to the young Portuguese – 'I often do that. Jane has no sense for such things.'

'If I come now you can tell me,' offered Jane a little tightly.

'Two women in one room dressing together?' April, who had shared her room with Jane all her life in their modest flat in Sydney, threw up her hands.

'It's a suite, not a room,' said Jane.

'All the same, darling, after the space we've been used to—' She shuddered. 'No, I'll leave your frock in readiness.'

When she had gone Rodriguez took Jane to see the lotus pool, for Jane had never seen lotus before in her life, only read about them.

'Actually they're much better in Burma. Also there they play a bigger role in temple worship than here, but they are lovely, aren't they?'

Jane bent over and touched the almost unbelievably satin petals, some pink, some white.

'We'll sit here if you like,' said Rodriguez, 'unless you would sooner the cooled lounge.'

'I love the sun.'

'You don't find it oppressive?'

'Why, no. I'm Australian, remember.'

'April finds it too much. She would like us to live in Portugal after we marry.'

'Would you?'

Rodriguez said a little uneasily, or Jane somehow

sensed it was uneasily, 'We must see, of course. It all depends.'

He did not say on what it depended, so Jane changed the subject and at the same time broached the subject of the airport again. She definitely did not want to go.

Rodriguez insisted what he had insisted before. 'Also,' he finished, 'you gave your word. Why are you so reluctant, Jane?'

'It was unplesant last night arriving and not being met,' mumbled Jane unwillingly.

'But,' reminded the young Portuguese gently, 'that was your fault. You never told April when you were coming, so how was she to know?'

It was such a silly little lie it was not worth correcting, all the same it irritated Jane sufficiently to prompt her to announce: 'But for Mr. Marsden I would have been in a spot.'

As Rodriguez frowned, she asked, 'Why are you so antagonistic to Terry Marsden? April was quite livid when he brought me here.'

'April appreciates the position,' said Rodriguez with a formality that sat rather absurdly on him. 'Actually' – relaxing a little – 'I like the fellow, but to many people in Colombo he is quite beyond the pale. In April's and my position we both feel we must be careful.'

Jane said forthrightly, 'Why? You love each other. You intend to marry. What else is there? What else to concern anyone but yourself and April?'

'Quite a deal.' Rodriguez admitted.

Jane was nonplussed. She could not understand her sister's attitude, to dislike anyone who did not come up to her personal standards, and undoubtedly Terry Marsden would never come up to her standards, was simply April.

But she could not understand Rodriguez. He was young. He was easy-going. In his own words he 'liked the fellow.' Yet he practised a caution that was foreign to him, though a caution that came instinctively to April. There was something here that Jane could not understand.

She became aware that Rodriguez was looking at her, wetting his lips preparatory to saying something.

But it was not to be said. At that moment April came down the broad staircase . . . a more effectual entry than from the lift . . . and the silk suit was glowing pink, not the colour for a hot climate, not the colour for flame hair, but on April simply superb in spite of everything.

While Rodriguez was struggling for words, Jane went upstairs. A grey cotton with a demure white collar was laid out. Jane regarded it, then said aloud, 'But you're wrong, April. I'm a brown wren, not a grey mouse.'

She was past caring, however, and got into it without bothering to check her reflection, which was a pity, for that reflection would have lent her confidence, would have explained the pout that again settled on April's full red lips.

'We will go now,' decided Rodriguez, and they got into his car, a good car but not lavish, observed Jane. She observed that April was observing this, too.

It was not a gay journey to the airport. April was still pouting, still observing the less-than-luxury car, Rodriguez was preoccupied and not very cheerful, Jane was frankly hating going into the terminal again.

But three reluctant people made no difference to the turning wheels. The wheels still bore you there, bore you through narrow streets sometimes thronged so thickly that you literally had to inch your way through the crowds, bore you past afforestations that Rodriguez said were jaggery palm that yielded a sort of rough brown sugar from its sap, bore you through orchards of limes, shaddocks, grenadillas and plantains.

It would all have delighted Jane had she not felt so

oddly heavy ... prescient ... as though something was going to happen.

What could? Everything that might occur, that is everything unpleasant, or at least unfortunate, already had occurred. Until her sister married her Rodriguez, or departed for Portugal to marry him, Jane felt she had had her share of misfortune, or misdirection, sufficient unto the day, and the week, and the month.

Rodriguez parked the car and they entered the building. It looked different by daylight, brighter, less foreign. Nonetheless Jane averted her eyes from the coffee lounge, from the wall against which Terry Marsden indolently had leaned.

'Flight 17 from Madras,' intoned a voice, and Rodriguez said, 'This will be it. It's a domestic line – Air-Colombo.'

Now the unease was really disturbing Jane, her hands were damp, but her throat was dry and tight.

'Jane, are you all right? You look ghastly. You shouldn't have sat like that in the sun.' It was April and she seemed a long way away.

'I'm all right. Of course I'm all right,' Jane said – but only with her lips. She was far from all right. How could she feel right with that man coming from the tarmac through the terminal door?

He was tall, broad, olive-skinned, infinitely suave, he had a small moustache. Jane did not need April's quick little intake of breath to tell her that Rodriguez's uncle was much taller, much broader, much more blandly attractive than his nephew who had left their side to hurry across.

For he must be the uncle. Who else? Rodriguez had gone straight to him, taken his hand. He was leading him back.

Had she not been so concerned with herself, with the last time she had seen this man, Jane might have

70

found a little wry amusement in April's gasped, 'But I thought he'd be old!'

Old and doddering, had been April's words. Some-one whom she intended to put in his place the moment she married the young nephew.

But it was April who was being put in her place — coolly, formally, ever so politely. *But in her place.* With the barest click of his heels Senhor Camoes took April's hand and brushed his lips over the white skin. He took his time over the gesture, but one had the impression that it was because he would always be unhurried, not because he wished to eke out the salute.

But, realized Jane with shamed certainty, as at last he stepped back then turned to her, it was neither a roman-tic nor unhurried nature that had made him take his time over April, it was a reluctance to greet the sister.

The click of the heels was the same. The salutary brush of the lips on a sunburned, square-nailed hand this time, the same. But the eyes . . .

The eyes challenged hers.

CHAPTER FOUR

THEY were in Rodriguez's car and drawing away from the airport. Jane had only a confused idea of the sequences that had taken place after Senhor Camoes had released her hand, stepped back to bow briefly, coolly, again, then turned to his nephew.

The actions had been like the flick in a deal of cards, like the quickly turning facets of a kaleidoscope. She had been aware of a porter taking the senhor's bags, of Rodriguez saying, 'The car is waiting,' of a faintly uncertain April ... uncertain for the first time in her life? ... moving forward, and she, Jane herself, moving mechanically as well.

As they had crossed the terminal another card had flicked. It had been Terry Marsden – not leaning indolently this time but sitting lazily, legs pushed out, his notebook in his hand. He had waved the book airily to the party and April, by Jane's side, had visibly stiffened. Rodriguez had saluted back, Senhor Camoes had inclined his head formally, and Jane given a rather wobbly smile, at least she believed that that was what had happened. The turning facets of the kaleidoscope had been too quick for her to be certain.

At the car there had been a small delay as the bags were stowed and the party seated.

For Rodriguez, who was driving, there was no arrangement, but April had stood hesitant ... also for the first time in her life? ... not knowing whether to climb in with her Roddy, or sit at the back.

For the briefest of moments Joao Camoes had kept them waiting. Would he get in the rear with April where he could further the acquaintance? April's eyes had lit

up. Or in the back with Jane, leaving April to sit with her
fiancée-to-be, thus establishing his approval of the
match? Again .... though with slightly *less* enthusiasm,
Jane saw . . . April glinted.

But the senhor did neither. Politely he helped the
ladies in, April first, Jane next, then he seated himself
beside Rodriguez. The car edged off.

A quick glance at her half-sister had disturbed Jane.
There was a look on April's beautiful face that she had
seen before. It had been the time she had brought Jeff
home to the flat, and April . . . April . . .

April was looking at the two men in front of her, and it
had not needed Jane's experience to know that April was
comparing, that she was weighing up, that she was
reaching a sum total that was causing two little creases
across her usually smooth white brow.

Jane regarded the men herself. Joao Camoes was far
taller, far broader than Rodriguez Carreras, he was much
more mature. There was also an air of worldly assurance
about him that had not settled yet on Rodriguez's
slighter, younger shoulders, an experience, a wisdom, an
unmistakable and unarguable affluence. A subtle superiority, and not only in the impeccable cut and material of
his formal lounge suit as compared to Roddy's more
casual attire, but in the man himself.

Jane saw that now there were three creases on April's
brow.

She tried to turn her attention to the scenery – after
all this was new, fresh country – but her eyes kept coming
back to the two men seated in front of her . . . and to
April.

Presently Senhor Camoes began speaking in Portuguese to Rodriguez Carreras, asking, of the back seat,
formal permission first.

'Perhaps you will appreciate the fact that we have
many business things to say,' he explained. 'I have been

overnight and early morning in Madras ironing out a problem, and naturally I can discuss the result with my nephew more flexibly in my own tongue.'

'Of course,' smiled April, to whom the apology had been addressed. Jane, since he had not even looked at her, said nothing. She heard the smooth interchange of words she could not understand; a rather musical and flowing language this Portuguese, she decided.

April had stopped weighing up the situation and was weighing herself up instead, looking in her handbag mirror, adjusting here and there, ridding her brow of the three creases. When Senhor Camoes turned to speak in English again she was beautiful, serene and smooth-browed.

'We will take you to your hotel and the four of us have luncheon there,' said Joao Camoes. 'You are in which hostelry, senhorita?'

'Shangri-la.' Rodriguez said it for April.

'So.' There was no frown on the senhor's brow, but there was an enigmatical look in his dark eyes that did not escape Jane – or April.

April wetted her lips with the tip of her tongue prior to saying something. Then, after a moment's thought, she said nothing. It was that unrevealing 'So', that enigmatical look, that silenced her. She did not know whether to explain the Shangri-la, whether to praise or regret it. Or, Jane knew, too, whether to put it all down as a whim of her sister's, which, for April, would be her expected form.

She must have decided to bide her time, see how things went, for, when Rodriguez's car was put in the Shangri-la porter's hands to be driven away and garaged, she followed the men docilely into the big hotel, Jane a little to her rear.

Last night Jane had been a little aghast at the obvious luxury of the hotel, now she found herself more aghast at the too-lavish displays, the too-apparent affluence, the slight trend to the showy and the ostentatious. Her sister was no fool, she sensed it as well. And she realized what had been meant in the senhor's 'so'.

Softly, yet loud enough to be heard by the man in front, she said to Jane, 'Darling, why did you? We were quite comfortable enough before. This place is – well!'

Rodriguez took no notice, he was looking for a steward to arrange a table, but Joao Camoes could not help but overhear.

Jane wondered what his reaction would be to the ornate dining room, but a few words in Portuguese must have ordered Rodriguez as to his requirements, for when the party was bowed in it was to a small, more subdued, private annexe, much less marble to it, a more sober decor, only one fairly simple arrangement of flowers – Temple flowers. In Australia they were called frangipanni. They gave up their faint, sweet temple air. Jane went across to smell the gentle breath, and over the creamy flowers with their golden hearts she looked up to meet the eyes of Joao Camoes. April and Rodriguez were standing by the window together. They were saying something in soft voices, they were absorbed in each other. For a moment the senhor and Jane were quite alone.

'You were not,' observed the Portuguese in his formal voice but a much lower voice now, 'so anxious to meet the Senhor Marsden this time, Senhorita Winter. Not a disagreement, I trust? Not what the English, so no doubt the Australian, calls a tiff?'

Jane had time to reply only a bare 'No' before April and Rodriguez turned. But even if she had had the opportunity what else had she to answer to what he asked?

The table was set and the meal was brought in. Jane had the impression that it was simpler than customary but more meticulously and fastidiously served. The waiters moved silently and carefully, and but for their frequent anxious glances at the Senhor Camoes they might have been automatons.

That he was not the ogre that undoubtedly their superiors had warned them was borne out by a rupee note that he handed across between the final red wine and the coffee. Jane, not yet used to Sinhalese rupees, could still tell by the pleased faces that it was a substantial reward for their services.

'Thank you,' they bowed.

The table was cleared, only the coffee appointments left. April poured gracefully, aware that a woman can look her most charming attending to such rites.

At first the conversation was desultory, and then it became more pertinent. Senhor Camoes inquired from April how she had come to Colombo, evincing interest when she said by ship. Which ship? followed. The weather, the ports of call. Had Senhorita Winthrop liked Singapore ... for the briefest of moments Joao Camoes was looking not at April but Jane.

Soon ... any moment ... he would say, 'But your sister did not sail, she flew. In the same plane as I flew,' and April's turquoise eyes would widen, then narrow. Narrow on Jane.

Jane felt she could not wait for that. She wished desperately that she had told April last night, but then how could she? She had not known then that Senhor Camoes ...

'If I may be excused I'll go upstairs.' Jane rose, rose definitely before she could be stopped by any protests, by more coffee, by being sucked into a new conversation. The two Portuguese gentlemen got to their feet and bowed. April did not protest. Handling two men by herself rather pleased her.

But when she came up to the suite half an hour later,

Jane back at the window trying to be diverted as she had been diverted this morning, April was not pleased. So Joao Camoes had wasted no time telling her!

But April's first words refuted this. Had she been told April certainly would not have started first on another strain.

'I don't know what to think,' she began rather in a wail. 'I really don't. What's your impression, Jane?'

'Impression?'

'Of Joao Camoes, of course, who else? He's certainly not what I thought, not what Roddy gave me to expect.'

'Did Rodriguez really give any impression, April, or did you build one up yourself?'

'Well, I ask you, *an uncle*!'

'An uncle can be even younger than a nephew,' reminded Jane.

'Joao is older,' April said reflectively, her eyes glinting again. 'I like a mature man,' she said definitely, and Jane shrank – for Rodriguez. April had said exactly the same words just before the Jeff episode had come to an end.

'Definitely he liked me,' said April.

'Then that augers well for you and Rodriguez.'

'I wasn't thinking of that.' Now April's voice was a little short of a wail again. 'Jane, you have to help me.'

'How?'

'Find out about Joao . . . what exactly he is in this firm of Roddy's. It could be he's as important as Roddy, I mean – well, I mean Roddy's "sir" each time he addresses him.'

'That could be Portuguese respect,' suggested Jane.

'It could be, and yet – Oh, I don't know.' April went restlessly round the room, picking things up, putting them down again. 'I wish—' she said helplessly.

Jane had a fair idea of what she wished, but she could not be worried about it, she had her own wish on her

mind, the wish that she had confided in April before Joao
Camoes eventually did.

One thing ... *now* ... she could not let the pretence
go on any further.

'April,' she said clearly, 'Mr. Camoes and I had met
previously. We came on the same plane.'

'Well, obviously you didn't impress him,' shrugged
her sister. 'He didn't even recognize you.' She was still
self-absorbed.

'But he did,' gulped Jane. 'He spoke about Terry
Marsden ... asked why I was not so anxious to meet him
this time.'

Now April's attention was on Jane. She looked at her
furiously, and Jane's heart sank. April had a quick, sharp
temper.

'What do you mean? Tell me at once. You mean to say
that you flaunted this man in front of him? What did you
say to Joao on the trip up? That is' – sarcastically – 'if
you did speak.'

'We sat together.'

'You ... Oh, so that's it, is it? You're trying to warn
me hands off.'

'Hands off? April, what on earth—'

'You could see, as I could see, too, that Joao – that
Rodriguez – that Joao – Oh, you're the sly one, Jane. So
you flaunt that man, that Terry Marsden, to start me
off in a bad light!'

'If what you suppose was true,' pointed out Jane
reasonably, 'wouldn't it be I who was in the bad light?'

April absorbed that and brightened slightly. Because
she had to live the next few weeks with her half-sister,
and because she knew from experience that unless one
lived fairly amicably life could be unbearable, Jane took
advantage of the brightening and said, 'I'm sorry for anything that has happened, April. Believe me, none of it was
intentional, I wouldn't have embarrassed you for the

world. If I can help you now I'll be glad to do so. I like Rodriguez very much and I'm sure—'

But now April was darkening again, losing the smile in her turquoise eyes.

'Just forget Roddy for a while,' she said, 'and find out about Joao. I mean I can hardly go and ask – ask—'

'Ask what?'

'If he's married, engaged. The most important of all—'

'Yes?'

'What he is? Whether he could be what I think he could be, and I can tell you, Jane, that if he is—'

April went across to the window from which Jane had withdrawn and for quite a while did not speak. But when she did her words shocked Jane, though, she thought drearily, she should have expected them.

She said, fastening down her bottom lip with her white, even teeth:

'I never did like young men, and Rodriguez Carreras is very young, quite immature – almost a boy. But Joao Camoes—'

Words were on Jane's lips, words like, 'April, you're not going to drop Rodriguez like you dropped Jeffery, are you? Drop him because all at once somewhere else the fields are greener?' But she never uttered them. For one reason she was a little afraid to, for all her instinctive feelings for the young and obviously in-love Portuguese, afraid of April's anger. The other reason she held her tongue was because April gave her no chance to do otherwise. She monopolized the conversation, examining Jane closely as to her trip and what had taken place between her and the Senhor Camoes.

'Nothing did.' Jane remembered the tour of the shops at Darwin, their mutual, hers and the senhor's, admiration of the opal bracelet. His gift of a koala bear. She told April about the bear in case she found it, and inquired, and April said rather sharply, 'An odd gift. Are you sure there was nothing else? What did you talk about on the journey?'

'Very little. You see, I slept.'

At that April tossed back her red-gold hair and laughed delightedly.

'You are a strange girl, Jane – you sit beside this Joao Camoes and what do you do? Sleep. Now I'm beginning to believe your job with Max Everett was just that after all, a job.'

'What else?'

'Darling, from six to eleven every night! Now you're angry. Please don't be, because I really love my little sister very much, and you know it, Jane.'

Jane did not know it, but she knew that she herself had a lot of affection, deserved or otherwise, for April. She knew April knew it, and would trade on it. And she, Jane, being vulnerable and unable to do anything about it, would let her have her way. But not the way she wanted now. She would *not*, she thought, pump Joao Camoes.

She said so definitely, and April shrugged.

'Perhaps you're right, it might give him ideas that you yourself are interested. 'I'll get it out of Roddy. I wonder what those two men are talking about down there. I was practically sent up here like a small child. That Joao is certainly used to authority.' April gave a little moue that was not entirely displeasure. 'We'll soon find out!'

They found out within the hour. A message came up that the senhor would like to see the Senhorita Winthrop in the coffee lounge.

'Why can't he come up here?' pouted April; she had put on a very charming negligee.

'He mightn't approve of that, nor approve of Rodriguez coming, either.'

80

'Oh, Roddy!' April was flicking back her frocks ... a large collection of frocks, much larger than the number she had brought from Sydney. She chose a cool lime with a narrow white belt. White sandals, and she was ready.

'You do look lovely, April. But that dress—'

'Singapore, darling. They measure you and deliver the frock to the ship.'

'Was it expensive?'

'Their clothes are ridiculously cheap. That's why I bought so many.'

'So many? But, April—'

'Jane, don't fuss. It was essential.'

'I can't see why. At that time you hadn't met Rodriguez.'

'Please don't keep on about Roddy.' April was irritated. 'I've been bidden to go down to see Joao Camoes, Jane. Doesn't that indicate anything?'

'No,' said Jane.

'Well, *you* haven't been asked, have you, for all your advantage of knowing him first.'

Jane, nettled, said, 'I think he's asked to see you because you are senior. I think he has something to say.'

Now it was April who was nettled. She was always sensitive to being a year older.

'We'll see,' she smiled blandly, giving her hair a last flick.

Jane went with her to the door. 'April, I don't want you to tell any more lies about me – not to Senhor Camoes.'

'Why not to him more than anyone else?' April's eyes were narrowed. 'Anyway,' she defended, 'I told no lies.'

'Not directly, but you indicated that I'd been responsible for the change of hotels.'

'Darling, you're too sensitive. It was just something to say, I hate hollow silences. Besides, all's fair. Remember, Jane?'

'You mean' – Jane looked incredulously at her – 'all's fair in love and war?'

April nodded wickedly, her eyes laughing. She looked quite irresistible, Jane thought.

'But you love Rodriguez, April—'

'Of course, darling, and to win him I had to butter up Uncle.' April's evasion was butter-smooth, for she had not, and Jane had known it, been thinking in that strain.

'Cheer up, Janey.' April kissed her lightly. 'I have a feeling I'm getting somewhere at last. And' – with smiling promise – 'where I go my little sister comes, too.'

'Now to find out a few things. Why Joao is Camoes but Rodriguez Carreras.'

'We're Winthrop and Winter, remember,' said Jane.

'But not aunt and niece. Also, Joao's position, marital and otherwise.'

'Otherwise?'

'In the firm, silly. Wish me luck, Jane.'

'Luck?' Jane looked at her a little stupidly. Why would April need luck? But before she could question her, she was gone.

Jane spent the time until she came back tidying her clothes. There were literally rows of them. How much money could April have left of the joint sum that she and her mother had raised for her?

She unpacked a few things of her own, taking out the koala bear and putting the furry souvenir in the wardrobe. She cleaned April's shoes in the hope that if they were bright and attractive it might encourage April to hold on to them longer.

April came in at last in fair to moderate spirits.

'He's a close one,' she shrugged, 'but I've discovered he's not married. I explained our half-sistership, so he was obliged to explain the Camoes and Carreras. Roddy is the son of his older sister. Much older, I'd say, for Joao isn't all that much senior to Roddy. He's really a quite fascinating young-old.'

As Jane did not comment, she went on with her report.

'I don't know what he is in the firm, he was very cagey, but I'd guess he's some sort of adviser to Roddy. In which case—'

So Rodriguez was on again, Jane thought.

'Yes,' said April reflectively, 'I think that could be it. I think Roddy's "sir" is, as you suggested, Jane, just Portuguese formality. I feel nearly sure about his being an adviser, because already he's advised ... no, one could say *ordered* ... us to go to another hotel.' April tossed airily, 'So you can begin to pack, Jane.'

'But – but we've – I mean you've changed once already.'

'On your insistence, Jane.' April went into peals of laughter, reminding Jane of her implication earlier to-day, but, at a look in Jane's face, became instantly repentant.

'I'm sorry, Janey, but you know how important all this is to me. I could see how Joao despised the Shangrila, so what else could I do?'

'But Rodriguez didn't despise it.'

'No,' agreed April quite calmly.

Jane looked levelly at her half-sister.

'April, who is it you want?' she asked directly.

April was hunting round for words. If they had been honest words they would have been, 'The highest bidder.' But April did not deal in honesty.

'How can you ask such a question, Jane?' she reproached plaintively. 'You know how essential it is that I stand high in the family regard.'

'Meaning you lied only for Rodriguez?'

'Jane, don't fuss – unless it's over clothes. The taxi will be around in an hour.'

'Where are we going?'

'Some very select and elegant and no doubt as dry as dust hotel in the other end. But I rather think' – April fastened her teeth over her bottom lip – 'it won't be for long.'

'How do you mean?'

'There was a mention' – now April's turquoise eyes were glowing – 'of going up to the Hills. That's where all the people who matter go, Jane, to take the air.' She did a graceful little dance. 'Oh, I do love mattering, don't you?'

But Jane stood stolid. 'Where would we stop?'

'Joao's bungalow – or so I gathered. Oh, for goodness' sake get a move on, darling, the taxi will get here before we're ready.'

Jane gathered up some clothes and began to fold them. Typical of April, she went to the window, not offering to help. Still, thought Jane, just to have her in a good mood is all I ask.

Then April was speaking quite furiously, her good mood gone.

'That man is in the courtyard and he actually had the nerve to look up and wave. Oh, I could choke him! If Joao happened to see him he would be quite livid.'

'What man?' Jane was tucking in shoes nows.

April's reply made her glance up quickly, not because April said 'Terry Marsden' because Jane rather had expected Terry's name, but the manner in which April said it.

A manner angry beyond all proportion for the simple act of waving, furiously angry – yet something else as well. Somewhere in it a protesting, a futile, almost Jane could have said, a *desperate* note.

Desperate! Why desperate? Jane had never known a man yet whom April could not file in his allotted drawer.

The Senhor Camoes might prove the exception, but then Joao Camoes was exceptional himself. But Terry Marsden ... well, he was definitely run-of-the-mill. A rogue undoubtedly ... she, Jane, personally found him a likeable rogue ... but certainly never a threat to an intelligent, and April was extremely intelligent, girl.

Jane had pondered over it all as she had finished the packing, had received the call to proceed down to the lobby, had crossed the city to their new headquarters.

The Sterne Hotel proved just what April had said, very select and very elegant. But April never mentioned the dry as dust, because Joao Camoes himself conducted the girls there, saw them established.

'It's charming,' April said dutifully of the very chaste ... for the tropics ... building. 'Such refinement, so much quieter than the Shangri-la.'

Undoubtedly it was much quieter. There were no courtyards noisy with gay diners seated under gaudy sun umbrellas, no marbled bars bearing the names of Rainbow ... Kismet ... Nemesis ... where young ladies could sit and toy with long exciting drinks. Instead darkened cooled rooms were set aside for tea-taking, and a quick glance told Jane that even over tea a young lady did not sit alone. There were no bands and no glittering uniforms, only soft-footed calm and faultless service. And no fabulous red carpet.

However, when April came up to their suite after thanking the senhor she was not as irritable as Jane had expected. At least, not at first.

She said, 'By no means could you call it madly exhilarating, but I'd say there's not one guest here who is far from a millionaire.'

'April, how are we—'

'Jane, don't bother me with details. I told you it was only a brief stay.'

'But even a day here—' protested Jane.

'Darling, even your dim brain must have absorbed by now that I've been "accepted." In which case doesn't it only stand to reason that I must be especially protected, particularly when my protector is Portuguese? I really mean, Jane, everyone knows the fastidiousness of the Portuguese, how they guard their fair sex.

Jane said directly, '*Which* Portuguese?'

What her half-sister would have answered to that, either a sharp rebuke, a bantering rejoinder, or the stark truth with which April occasionally surprised you, Jane would never know, for there was a knock on the door. At a nod from April Jane answered it.

Terry Marsden stood there.

Because their suite had its own tasteful sitting-room, Jane asked the journalist in, receiving black looks from April as she did.

'You didn't take long to cross half of Colombo.' April opened the encounter in the rude manner she could when she chose to.

The newspaperman was quite unperturbed. 'As long as you did,' he drawled. 'I tailed you.'

'Well, what do you want?' April asked next.

'The routine things, Miss Winthrop.' Terry smiled blandly. 'How, when, where and why. Don't' – as April looked quite thunderous – 'take this as personal. I cover the Sterne along with the Shangri-la, Kandy, Galle and Grand Oriental. If I failed to write you up as a Sterne guest I'd be out on my ear.'

April said pointedly, 'Again.'

Terry smiled implacably, 'Again.'

'Don't you ever want to settle anywhere?'

'Don't you?'

'I'll be settling quite soon.'

The journalist took up his notebook. 'Can I quote you on that?' He paused ... rather diabolically, Jane thought ... 'And can I say – with whom?'

Jane had asked almost the same question, but it was different for a sister. She was in sympathy with April when April fairly threw him out of the room, if a slender girl could throw a large man like Terry.

Following after the reporter, Jane said reproachfully, 'You deserved that, you know.'

'I know.' He grinned. 'I apologize to you, Janey, but not to her. I know how she ticks. I should do, I tick rather the same way myself. We're both one of a sort. She was not so much insulted as furious at being found out, found out in the waiting game, waiting to know which one will make The Bid.'

'Which one?'

'Of the Portuguese gents.'

'You're quite wrong,' defended Jane. 'Already Rodriguez—'

'I refer to the bid that matters,' said Terry smoothly. 'Believe me, honey, one bid matters much more than the other, and I think that's what our lovely April is after.'

'Do you know the answer?' asked Jane pleadingly.

'What, want to do a spot of fishing yourself? No, take that back, kid. You're not the sort. You're only asking for your sister. Yes, of course I know. Everyone here knows.'

'Will you tell me?'

'Whether Rodriguez has the money or Joao? No, I won't. Let April do the dirty work.'

'The trouble is—' began Jane, then stopped. She had been about to say, 'The trouble is she expects the information from me.' But she was too loyal to admit that.

She need not have bothered. Terry laughed at her, lit a cigarette, called, 'See you in the information library, Janey,' waved an indolent arm and left.

When Jane returned to the suite, April was sitting at the phone, and she looked pleased again.

'We're all running out to Mount Lavinia, Jane.'

'All?'

87

'Joao, Roddy, both of us.'

'I really think I should stop here and write to Mother,' demurred Jane. 'She'll be anxious for news.'

'No news yet, so why waste time and postage? You are asked, too, and I'm glad of that. A threesome is an awkward number. I'll probably need you to take Roddy off my hands.'

'Rodriguez?' echoed Jane.

'Yes. I'll have to get what I want out of Joao myself, seeing you won't.'

'Can't you ask Rodriguez straight out?'

'I've tried, and he hems. No, I'll go direct to the source.'

In preparation April ran to her as yet unpacked case and began selecting a dress.

Jane, remembering Terry Marsden's description of Mount Lavinia ... 'creamy surf, coconut trees, everyone's dream of a tropical paradise come true' ... thought her sister's choice of a nasturtium silk shift very apt. For herself, she did not bother, save to remove the jacket of the brown and white striped cotton suit she had worn for the trip across town.

April carefully painted on an exactly matching nasturtium mouth, loosened her lovely flaming hair to a shoulder-length silken sweep, then went to stand by the window to watch for the men.

'This is certainly a very dull hotel,' she pouted presently.

'Millionaires notwithstanding?' teased Jane.

'I expect that's an exaggeration, and that they're only very rich. No doubt Mount Lavinia will prove an exaggeration, too.'

'I don't think so. Terry—' Jane remembered how April loathed Terry Marsden, so did not finish. But as Terry's words concerning the beach resort flashed back again there came another flashback – *that April would have liked.*

Were it true ... But Jane could not believe it was true. It was just *Senhor*, not *Count* Joao Camoes.

She became aware that April had turned her attention from the window to her sister. The turquoise eyes were speculative.

'What are you thinking about, Jane?'

Jane wondered a trifle hysterically what April's reaction would be if she announced: 'Portuguese Counts.'

April, fortunately not waiting for an answer, went on a little querulously, 'I don't feel I know you like I used to. I'm beginning to think it wasn't such a good idea bringing you here.'

Before Jane could remind her that she had brought herself on an award, also brought a further sum to help her sister, April snapped, 'What have you done to that dress?'

'This dress?' Jane was startled.

'What other? Have you altered it or something?'

'I've removed the jacket.'

April stared a long, rude moment, then turned to the window to look out again. What had happened to Jane? she was thinking. Plain Jane. Acorn brown Jane. April's long nails pinched into her palms. For one thing, she resented, Jane wasn't having the make-up trouble that she was, her powder did not streak in the humidity for the simple reason that she wasn't wearing any. The child had always had a good skin – her sole asset, really. April brightened a little and decided to be magnanimous. Jane could be very helpful, she reminded herself.

'You look quite nice,' she praised, 'but you want brightening. Wear my crystals.'

Jane did not want the crystals. They were triple-stringed and glittering and they did not suit the simple brown and white stripe.

'Wear them,' April insisted, fastening the clasp.

At that moment there was a soft knock on the door,

a soft voice informing the ladies that the gentlemen were waiting, so Jane left it at that.

When they descended to the Sterne courtyard ... no gay umbrellas and playing fountains, just stone benches under clipped shade trees ... it was to a long sports model instead of the car that Rodriguez had driven. And Joao Camoes was at the wheel. He wore an open-necked shirt of dull cream silk, but at the throat he had tucked a pale cinnamon cravat that almost blended in with the very deep olive of his skin. His hair, sleek and shining, was brushed immaculately back. His teeth gleamed white below the small clipped moustache. He looked, thought Jane, aware by April's erect stance by her side that her sister was thinking the same, relaxed, assured ... vitally alive.

In comparison Rodriguez Carreras appeared a little untidy ... hair blown, tie carelessly knotted. Or was it the air of Rodriguez that gave this impression? He seemed a little ill at ease, somehow. Unsure.

To April's undoubted delight she was beckoned in to sit beside Joao. Actually relieved, for she felt she could not have found anything to say to the Senhor Camoes, Jane got in beside the much more approachable ... well, she found it so ... Rodriguez. They set off.

The skyline enchanted Jane; it was almost fairylike, even though, as Rodriguez archly pointed out, some of the silhouette was supplied by twentieth-century radio towers that were intermingled with the old mosques.

Nearer to earth it was less enchanting. There was squalor here, overcrowding, and yet, Jane noticed, infinitely impressed, the children were beautiful, the women walked in grace and the men in pride. And they smiled.

'I love it,' she said impetuously, and Rodriguez looked incredulous.

But the Senhor Camoes turned briefly in the driver's seat, so briefly his eyes barely left the road, and looked at Jane. Jane knew she must have been mistaken when she thought afterwards in retrospect that those dark eyes had glowed at her.

They passed rickshaws and ox-carts, and once a double-decker red London bus that Rodriguez explained would have been bought second-hand. It was only a matter of some eight miles to Mount Lavinia, but every yard to the splendid headland Jane found quite fascinating ... then when the beautiful hotel loomed up, she was more charmed still. The eggshell blue and white she had seen on several Sinhalese edifices, but it was a loftier instance this time, pillared, terraced, many huge fans ensuring cooled air.

They went through the long corridor with the inevitable ... Jane already had discovered ... touts, or scouts, to clamour at you to patronize a certain shop. Joao dismissed them kindly enough but quite definitely, and veered his party to a cool terrace and a cooler lime squash.

Sipping it, April complained that the Colombo shopping was not like Singapore's.

'I saw only wooden flutes, suppercloths and baskets in the corridor "shops",' she shrugged, 'and the jewellery – why, it was only bean beads.'

Looking up from watching the ice growing smaller in her long frosted glass, Jane found Joao's eyes on her. Not really on her but on the glittering string that April had fastened round her neck. She flushed. She had known it was wrong, and undoubtedly this man, this immaculate, fastidious, knowledgeable man knew it, too. She lowered her gaze again.

The drinks finished, they walked by the beach. It was, thought Jane, dismissing her discomfiture, just as Terry had said, a dream of a tropical paradise come true. Some of the coconut palms grew right to the edge of the water, the graceful crowns wreathing rhythmically at each gentle breath of the salt wind. Under a tropical sun the sea took on a deeper brilliance, and the green vegetation of the headland interspersed with the trails of bright yellow sand made it inexplicably vividly beautiful.

Winsomely April had thrown off her sandals and run down to the creamy rim of the sea. Taking the sandals up, Rodriguez laughingly ran after her. Jane and Joao walked on, and presently they were in a small thicket of palms, nothing in sight except bending, swaying leaves, occasionally framing in deep sweet green an inch of brilliant blue sea. The only sound was the sough of the palm fronds and the sea wash, no human voice at all until Joao Camoes said: 'So you like Colombo, little Jane?'

'Yes.' Jane was a trifle confused, a trifle uncertain of herself at his low, rather teasing use of her name, but never uncertain of this pearl of an island. 'Oh, yes,' she said ardently again.

'I am glad of that. It is well that we are of the same mind.'

We? He was referring, of course, to April. As he was Portuguese, and almost fiercely family, or so Jane, through the intense respect of Rodriguez for his uncle, had gathered, the fact that she was April's sister, even though only a half-sister, was sufficient for him to include her.

'And this Mount Lavinia,' he asked. 'It, too, pleases you?'

'It enchants me.'

'Then you must have a memento of it.' He reached in his pocket to withdraw, unwrapped, a string of bean beads. A simple string, yet ... and Jane saw it at once ... the only adornment for the simple cotton dress she wore. Her hands went instinctively to her throat, foolishly trying to hide the wrong glitter of the triple swing that didn't belong there. She felt her cheeks burning.

'I think,' he said softly, 'that these will be right, little one. May I?' Without waiting for her permission he put his long, sensitive, olive-skinned hands round her neck and unfastened the clasp of the string she already wore. His fingers were cool – yet warm. The touch was cool. But the feeling, even after he had taken the hands, and the crystal necklet, away, tingled her skin.

He held out April's trinket to Jane and she took it. She stood quite still as he doubled the bean beads round her neck. No need for fingers to fasten this time. But they brushed her skin as they slid the string from their grasp, and again the touch was cool – yet warm.

'Ah, that is better.' He was standing back regarding her.

It was better. Cottage beads on a cottage dress for a cottage girl. Jane murmured it aloud.

'That is what you want, senhorita?' His voice held a rather odd, small concern, Jane thought. 'You want a cottage?'

'Yes.' She laughed, trying to hide the curious tension she felt building up in her. 'But I'll settle for a castle in Spain.'

'I can offer you neither,' he said quite solemnly, 'only a *palacio* in Portugal.'

'That sounds like a palace,' she laughed again, not taking him seriously. 'When did you buy these beads, senhor? I did not see any transaction.'

'A Sinhalese sale can be very quick so long as one does not bargain. I' – his eyes were rather narrowed on her now – 'never bargain. I know what I want and if it is there I pay the price.'

'Your price?'

'If I want it,' he persisted, 'I pay the price.'

Now was the time, thought Jane, while the subject was more or less to do with money, to find out what April wanted to know. But even if she had found the words Jane still could not have uttered them. She stood fingering her new necklace, aware of his deep look, so vividly aware

93

that at last she said a little agitatedly, 'I can't, of course, take these.'

His brows soared in question.

'These beads,' she explained.

The brows remained raised.

'It's very kind of you, but—' Her hands went up to uncoil the string, but at once his own hand shot up to prevent her.

'What is this? You took another gift.'

He meant the souvenir bear. But that was different. Jane went to say so, but the words were not said. April and Rodriguez came through the palm thicket looking for them, April's lovely face a study even before her sharp glance fell on the bean beads.

Something has angered her, Jane thought. She found out what it was the moment the door was closed on their suite at the Hotel Sterne. But before that she tackled Jane about the beads. She was furiously angry, even though Joao Camoes had arranged for a theatre party that night, a Sinhalese dance recital that sounded very exciting, and an invitation that April had accepted with charming enthusiasm.

But she was not charming now. She turned on Jane and took hold of the beads.

'Where did you get these?' she demanded.

'At Mount Lavinia.'

'I didn't see you buy them. Why did you waste your money? You already wore a very beautiful necklace. *My* necklace. Where is it? Did you lose it, Jane?'

'Here it is.' Jane handed it across. She said, hoping to appease April, 'The thing's only made of beans.'

But April was not to be appeased. The simple trinket on the simple dress did something for Jane, something that April could not put a finger on, and that fact infuriated her. Suddenly the cottage look, as Jane had said of herself, made everything else, and that included what

April wore, exaggerated and showy. In a burst of anger April pulled her hand down sharply and the next moment the beads were all over the floor.

With a little cry Jane went down on her knees to retrieve them, but as she crouched there she knew it was hopeless. She could never gather them all up, little more than seed-size as they were. Even if she did, she could not re-string them.

April at least had the grace to be sorry.

She said so, but added, 'Flimsy things, not worth worrying about. How much did you pay?'

'I didn't,' Jane said a little quickly. She was upset over the beads. 'The senhor bought them.'

'Joao?'

'Yes.'

'Bought them for you?' All at once — and fortunately — April decided to make a joke of it.

'First a teddy bear,' she scorned, 'then a string of bean beads. Kindergarten stuff!' She patted Jane's head, and the bean incident was closed. — Though in the closing Jane all at once remembered Joao Camoes saying when she had tried to reject the bean beads: 'What is this? You took another gift.'

But only of a bear, as April has just said. Kindergarten stuff. And yet, recalled Jane, he had looked very adult when he had reminded her of a previous bestowal. However, she did not have time to ponder over that look. Not then — for April was on another tack.

'I don't know what to think.' It was the old theme again. 'I worded Roddy, but as usual got no results. I don't know whether he has or has not. You know what I mean, Jane. Probably he has, but I'd like to know for sure. And I'd like to know how much it is in comparison to what Joao has.'

'April!'

'Oh, don't look so shocked. I bet you'd be interested yourself in finding out how many dollars ... no, pesetas or something, isn't it ... each of the Portuguese runs to. I know that Joao at least has this Hills bungalow, and that to have a Hills bungalow here, well—' She spread her hands. She went to the window ... a favourite spot when she had a problem.

'It's tricky,' she admitted. 'Joao could have only the bungalow and an income and Roddy could have the entire export firm. But on the other hand . . .'

She stood staring out on the courtyard. When she next spoke her voice had changed from concern to irritation, the same irritation as the last time she had stood at a window.

'He's there! That odious Marsden person. Writing up his little bits and pieces. There's a failure for you if you like. One thing' – a derisive laugh – 'there would be no choosing him.'

Jane, who had crossed to stand by April's side, looked down, too, on the journalist. From the courtyard below he looked back at them, then, almost as though he had heard April's scornful words, he shut his notebook, turned without acknowledging either of them and left.

CHAPTER FIVE

FOR some time afterwards Jane felt an odd little regret for the somehow bereft look of Terry Marsden leaving the Sterne Hotel. The sense of loneliness disturbed her, the air of failure and despair. His defences had been down, there had been no cocksure, don't-give-a-damn quirk, no bantering, no giving back as good as he was given.

'What a man!' April had taunted, and there had been no sympathy in her, only a leashed . . . barely leashed . . . anger. There was something, puzzled Jane, about the journalist that got under April's skin.

She wished she could dismiss Terry as apparently April dismissed him, with an uncaring shrug, but she couldn't. She kept seeing him again, hollow, empty . . . until a care of her own, not Terry's, took the spotlight.

It happened as she reached up to bring out her shoes to wear to the theatre. The bear that she had placed there tumbled down. Bending to retrieve him, her fingers closed on the soft grey fur . . . and on something else. Something she had not noticed before fastened round the soft bear neck. A bracelet. A bracelet of white opals. The bracelet that Senhor Camoes had examined at the Darwin airport, Jane felt sure of that, that he had invited Jane to examine as well. The bracelet of whose flashing depths of purple and gold in a milky sea he had said: 'The white opal would be for you.'

But how . . . *how* had it got here?

He had handed it to her to examine. Had she forgotten to give it back? But if this had happened how could it be fastened securely now round the neck of the bear? It could never have found its own place there. Jane looked again, double-checked. No, it was impossible. Not only was the clasp fastened but it was safety-chained as well.

At the same time that she suddenly ... and tremblingly ... recalled the senhor's comment at Mount Lavinia on her objection to the bean beads, that surprised: 'What is this? You took another gift,' April's enthralled voice, enthralled because of the opal bracelet, cut into Jane's painful recollection.

'That's quite exquisite! It's absolutely beautiful! How much did it cost? Where did you buy it?' A pause. Then, in a dangerous voice: 'Jane, did *he*—'

'No. No, of course not.' Jane knew she protested with her heart as well as her lips. He couldn't have ... He mustn't have ... And yet the bracelet was in her hands.

In April's hands really. Thank goodness Jane had removed the circlet from the bear's neck before her sister could see the meticulous care with which it had been fastened. Otherwise Jane's subsequent, 'I don't know how it got here. I'm very worried about it ... I saw a string like this in Darwin, but—' would have rung very hollow.

But now all April's response was a gay, 'Well, pet, don't worry. Darwin is Australia, and if the worst comes to the worst you can always explain.'

'Explain what?'

'How you came by it, and that is entirely by accident. Also you can explain in English, Jane, not struggle in Sinhalese. All I can say is: *Ma palathe nama mokakda* ... What is the name of this place? Joao taught me today, but it wouldn't be much use squaring off an opal bracelet, would it?' April laughed. She was pleased about the beautiful piece of jewellery. As Jane did not join her pleasure, she offered magnanimously, 'You're still worried! Look, I'll wear it tonight for you and break the ice.' Without waiting for Jane's permission she put it on, and, knowing April, Jane knew that that was the end, for her, of the opal bracelet. Still, she thought dreamily, though unconscious of dreaming, I have the bean beads, if not in my hands, then in my thoughts.

'They're not really my choice,' April was admitting. 'I go for the black opal, but this is such a beautiful piece, Jane.'

Remembering the sharp eyes of the senhor, anticipating the quick lift of his eyebrows as he saw the bracelet on April's slim wrist, dreading what he might comment but dreading more what April would say later, Jane appealed to her sister, if she must wear it, not to flaunt it.

'I feel guilty,' she explained.

'Poor darling, I never do. I promise I won't even lift my wrist. Anyone would think you'd been given it by a secret lover.'

'I wasn't given it at all,' said Jane, not knowing whether she spoke the truth or not, but feeling that surely she must be speaking it, for Joao Camoes might give her a cheap bean necklet, but never more than that, and yet – frowning – that lock and chain. The bear, she thought a little hysterically, could never have done that.

April was whisking out an emerald chiffon, pouting at a crease.

'Darling, could you—' she coaxed.

'Yes,' said Jane, needing occupation, diversion, 'I'll press it for you.' She took up the green filmy folds and went along to the laundry unit.

April, her dress attended to, her wrist adorned, was in an angelic mood. She cast Jane no reflective glances as Jane dressed, and the pearls she offered her for the unadorned white sheath that Jane pulled over her head were right.

Amicably the girls descended to the lobby. Even the quiet brownness of it, the lack of orchestra, pomp and show, did not discourage April. She was radiant when the men appeared, and Joao Camoes remarked on the radiance, bending gallantly to kiss her hand. It was, Jane observed thankfully, not the hand with the bracelet. Even though she knew she must broach the subject of the opal piece, she wanted to do it in a more tactful manner than April holding up her slender arm with the milky circlet of flashing stones.

A car was waiting and they sped through the darkling street to where the dance recital was to be held. In the lushness of the tropical night the seamier side of the overcrowded ways lost its squalor and became, with its lights, a Sinhalese version of the Arabian Nights.

At the theatre they were shown to comfortable stage-side seats, and almost at once the dance fiesta began.

First there were Indian dancers, resplendent in richly gemmed breastplates and Turkish trousers, and it was impossible not to be carried away by the slap of the drums that beat out the rhythm for their jewelled feet.

A Kandyan troupe performed next. This, whispered Joao Camoes to the girls, was one of the most ancient art forms in existence today.

'The dancing is still pure,' he explained, 'despite over a century of foreign contact.'

Jane watched in fascination at the graceful sinuous movements. It was totally different dancing from the Indian fiesta, it was more aesthetic.

A Devil, or Bali, dance brought the feast to the long interval. This was a dance of masks, ranging from kings to demons, and it depicted the barbaric and grotesque.

The dancers took their bows, the ornate curtains drew together, and the audience drifted out for cool drinks on an open terrace.

'It was delightful,' enthused April, 'though I must say I found the last one a little uncivilized.'

'It is supposed to represent faith in the supernatural. That is one of the characteristics of the Sinhalese villager

– a very inherent trait.' The senhor took out his cheroots, offering one to Rodriguez, who refused and instead lit up a cigarette. Joao took his time over his cigar, then said, 'Speaking of villagers brings the subject to where a villager lives.' He smiled slightly. 'A village, naturally.'

'Yes, Joao?' April's eyes were wide and shining, her red lips slightly apart.

'I wish you to experience a village.'

'Any special village?' It was April again, still waiting on his words.

'Yes, senhorita. Our own.' – *Our* own. So April was still not to find her answer. – 'Not actually our own, of course, but the grounds of Ambanta are so extensive that they comprise practically all the land, and, in maintenance, employ all the villagers.'

'Tea?' asked Jane in interest.

'Yes, senhorita. Also a little coffee, though after the coffee failure in the end of the last century tea is preferred by the planters. Also, seeing our estate is extensive, and in a small island like Ceylon one crop must come on top of another, there is as well some rubber and coconut. All this is not counting our strip of jungle where we have been emulating Burma and planting teak. Though' – with a smile – 'if you come, that part of Ambanta will be strictly taboo without Rodriguez or myself and several guides.'

'But why, Joao?' Once more April.

'This is still a wild island in parts,' related Joao. 'Aside from losing yourself in those forests of blackwood you could come face to face with a sloth bear, even a leopard. In the creeks, and there are many, a crocodile. In the grasslands which fringe the jungle even a rogue elephant.'

'A rogue?'

'A wild one. Ordinarily elephants cannot be shot without licences, and that is right, but with a rogue no permission is necessary.'

'It all sounds very fearsome,' said April.

'But wonderful.' Jane was not aware that she was sitting forward in her chair, her eyes like stars. She was soon brought to heel. Annoyed at the animated picture she made, at the men's rapt attention at Jane's almost little-girl thrall, deliberately April held up her hand with the opal bracelet on it, ostensibly to adjust her shining flame hair, but no doubt to break up the unpleasing ... to her ... tableau.

'That is a pretty piece,' Rodriguez admired of the bracelet.

April smiled. Joao said nothing.

They went back to the dance feast, to more beating feet, swaying bodies, and vibrant, thrilling booms of drums. They had coffee in a city restaurant, after which Rodriguez by devious, yet very obvious, methods managed to spirit April into a car of his own arranging instead of his uncle's. The look on April's face as he triumphantly bore her off was rather a study. Jane did not relish her sister's return to the hotel that night.

'The conquering hero looks very happy,' remarked Joao Camoes drily, 'but I would not say that about the conquered, would you?'

Jane answered uneasily, 'She was just taken by surprise.'

Thinking this could be an opening, Jane went on, 'As I was taken by surprise tonight, senhor. I was lifting down my souvenir bear when I found around its neck the opal bracelet that we were examining in Darwin. I have no idea how it got there, and I'm very upset. Do you think I could cable the firm?'

'For what reason, Miss Winter?'

'To ask them if – if—'

'If an opal bracelet has been stolen?'

'Mislaid,' substituted Jane.

He had been smoking his cheroot, but abruptly he put it down.

'You are not serious, surely?'

'Certainly I am.'

'You really want me to believe the bracelet took you by surprise?'

'It did, senhor.'

'You had not noticed it before?'

'No.'

'And even when you found it securely fastened and chained you still thought it could have got there by mistake?'

'I thought that unlikely, but – but how else?' Jane was distressed.

'This is quite unbelievable,' he frowned. 'You did not argue with me today at Mount Lavinia when I said that you must accept the bean necklace because you had accepted a gift before.'

'I – I thought you referred to the souvenir bear. Had I known, senhor, that an opal bracelet was included I certainly wouldn't have accepted that.'

'That I can believe,' he commented drily, 'for you have not accepted it now, you have passed it on to your sister. If you are so proper, senhorita, for yourself, why is it that you are not so careful for Miss Winthrop? Oh, I know she is not a full relation, but there is still a very close tie. As a Portuguese, I cannot understand this trait in you. To us family is everything; first the closer family, and then, like the aureoles of a circle, the kith, as you call it, and the kin.'

Nettled, Jane said, 'I won't argue about that, instead I will question the opal bracelet. Why did you buy it, senhor? Fasten it on the bear?'

'I could have wished to bring it here without paying Customs.' He yawned deliberately.

'But that wouldn't be true.' It would not, Jane knew. This man would be the last man in the world to use tactics to beat Customs, he would be far too arrogant, too formal, too proper. Besides, had he not said of himself that he never bargained? Anyway, Jane doubted if on a personal string of opals any penalty would be required to be paid.

'You are discerning, senhorita. No, I did not do it for that. The piece appealed to me, so I bought it. But gems like those must be worn, not stored, otherwise they lose their vitality, so I bought them. For you. For your own sake, since you are still very naïve, child, one could almost say gauche, I spared you the embarrassment of presenting them to you personally. I used' – he took up the cheroot again – 'our mutal friend the bear.'

'But – but, senhor, they were expensive.'

'I told you at the time a black string would be dearer.'

'Yet still quite a sum.'

The cheroot went down once more.

'There is something I must say to you, Jane, something I sense is very important to you' – a pause – 'and your sister. It is this: Money is of no concern to me. By that I do not mean I do not value and appreciate it, but rather that I have enough never to have to think about it. In other words' – he took up the cheroot, inhaled, exhaled almost lazily – 'I am well-situated.' A deliberate pause. 'I am rich.'

His black eyes sought and held hers, they probed, they extracted.

She knew she could not let this pass. 'What – what do you mean, senhor? To what are you referring?'

'You ask me that? You on whose lips such a question trembled today at Mount Lavinia. The question of my means.'

She was silent and ashamed. For the words *had* been there. The words – for April.

He watched her closely, reading her guilt, and his lips thinned.

'Now,' he said at length, 'you can rest assured that I am worth the bother.'

'Senhor!' she gasped.

'You can also inform your sister.'

'Really, Senhor Camoes—'

'Yes, Miss Winter?'

But Jane could not find the words. She sat infinitely troubled until, quite unexpectedly, very gently, he leaned across and touched her hand.

'There, little one, I am harsh with you. My real reason is that Rodriguez, of whom I am inordinately fond, has become restless of late, dissatisfied. Not only these things but as well very demanding.'

'Demanding?'

Joao Camoes smoked a moment.

'You must understand,' he said presently, 'that in a business like ours one must succeed slowly for a success to be established permanently. Rodriguez has recently wished everything at once on his plate.' Through the weave of smoke the black eyes searched Jane's. 'Would you know why?'

'Of course not, senhor.' Jane knew she protested too quickly.

A few moments went by in absolute quiet. Then the senhor shrugged: 'Well, at least you are Portuguese in that.'

'In what?'

'You protect your family.'

Jane got up abruptly, preparatory to leaving. Upon her rising he rose formally as well.

'You wish to go back already? But surely the young lovers will be later than this.'

'I wish to go, senhor. As for the young lovers, aren't you presuming?'

'If you say so.' He bowed. 'I had formed my opinion by my nephew's attitude. Rodriguez, to say the least, is extremely keen. Perhaps your sister will be equally keen when you assure her that as young men go Rodriguez is favourably placed.'

But that, knew Jane, would never satisfy April. Its range was too wide. It could mean just comfortable . . . or it could mean reasonably affluent. But could it mean, as Joao had said of himself, *rich*?

Probably Rodriguez as he grew maturer would become rich. But April . . . April had to have everything at once. Suddenly something seemed to turn in Jane's heart. Did April have to have it from this man now standing beside her, helping her with her wrap?

But Joao Camoes was scornful of April, derisive.

Almost eagerly, and she was ashamed of it, Jane said, 'You don't like my sister.'

'On the contrary' – his voice was undeniably warm – 'I admire her tremendously. She has quite fabulous beauty, and she is, I think, an honest person.'

Honest? April?

'She has come to terms with herself, which in a woman is refreshing and rare. You, for instance, look in a mirror but never in your heart.'

'Is that required?' Jane's voice was stiff. She did not understand this man . . . but she did understand that for all his arrogant criticism of April he was still deeply interested in her. She remembered how he had added to his information as to his own monetary standing: 'You can also inform your sister.'

Did that mean he wanted Jane to tell April that he – that he –

Joao Camoes broke into her thoughts with a cool, 'Tomorrow I will arrange for us to go to the Hills bungalow.'

'You are too kind, senhor.' She was equally cool.

'By no means kind. It is essential. Even if the family was not personally interested' – the family, noted Jane, not just Rodriguez – 'even if you were merely two young ladies in Colombo, I still could not allow you to remain here. And now' – before she could argue – 'I feel you might be later than Miss Winthrop, and that, for a younger sister, is not the thing.'

It certainly was not the thing. One look at April's face as Jane entered their Sterne suite told Jane that.

'Where have you been? Why were you so long? Why did you let Rodriguez monopolize me like that?'

'But, April, isn't that what you want?' Jane unfastened April's pearls and handed them back to her sister. 'Also we went nowhere.'

'Neither did we.' April was pouting. She was also troubled. 'I wouldn't have minded so much if Ruddy had gone on to some night club, but – ' She paced the room restlessly. 'Jane,' she said at last, 'I just don't think he has the money.'

'Then, darling' – Jane felt she'd better reassure her – 'he has.'

'You found out?'

'Yes.'

'He has money?'

'Yes, April, he has.'

But before Jane's eyes a strange thing was happening. Instead of being reassured, relieved, April seemed more troubled. She went to the window, came back. Jane had a shrewd idea of what she was thinking. She was wondering *how* much? How much compared to – to Joao Camoes?

But when April spoke it was of neither of the Portuguese gentlemen.

'He was in the lobby when we came in – that Marsden. Book, pencil and nothing else.' The laugh was a little harsh, slightly hysterical.

Then April repeated derisively:
'Nothing else.'

By ten the next morning they had left the Hotel Sterne
– and Colombo – for Joao Camoes' Hills bungalow in the
village of Ambanta.

To Jane's surprise it had been April who had held back
at the last moment, April to whom this very significant
move to a private abode Jane would have thought would
have comprised a considerable triumph. But April, even
while Jane had packed, had demurred.

'Don't you think several cases will be sufficient? We
could leave the remainder here at the Sterne.'

'I think Senhor Camoes wishes us to take all of them.'
Jane repeated to her sister what Joao had said to her.

He had stated definitely: 'Even if you were merely two
young ladies in Colombo I still could not allow you to remain here.'

'How dull,' said April.

'What do you mean – dull?'

'I don't mean Joao or Roddy, of course.' April's answer had been quick. 'But I do mean the Portuguese protection. Such a boring word, protection.'

'But, darling' – Jane had been worried, for after all, if
she married a Portuguese April must learn to agree as well
as decree – 'protection is one of their characteristics, and
if you're really serious—'

'Of course I'm really serious. What on earth gave you
the idea I was not serious.' Irritable – to Jane's idea –
beyond all proportion, April had fairly flung herself
across the room to stare moodily out of the window.

'It's all right for you,' she said presently, 'you'll be really
interested in all those barbaric things that Joao told us
about. You'll remark on the tea crop, the rest of the odious
industries, and mean it. I'll be near tears.'

'But being April won't show it,' said Jane with determined cheerfulness. 'Look at it this way if you can't raise any other enthusiasm: your make-up will remain perfect. You're always complaining of the stickiness here.'

But April was not to be jollied. She simply stood at the window while Jane finished the last case. But when, having been bidden by the hotel porter, the girls descended to the lobby, and the car into which they were ushered proved a larger and more expensive version than any that they had driven in yet, April began to become her old self.

Her quick, acquisitive turquoise eyes took in the quiet resplendency of the limousine, the immaculate uniform of the smiling Sinhalese who opened the door. She saw years of such service, such resplendency, her only immediate problem which of the two charming Portuguese would ensure the greater grandeur. Forgetting the boredom she had foreseen in Joao's Hills bungalow, April for the present chose the maturer man and stepped in beside him in the seat immediately behind the driver. Jane got in with Rodriguez in the rear compartment.

There were glass divisions, but they were not pulled up. Jane could hear April's gay chatter as the car travelled through the Colombo streets. She was temporarily silenced, however, as another car, a shabby sports model in London bus red, eased past them from the opposite direction.

'Terry Marsden,' said Rodriguez by Jane's side. 'He must be after a story.'

April was pulling out her cigarettes, fumbling with the lighting of one. With a little low laugh the Senhor Camoes took over and presently April looked her bland beautiful self again.

Jane turned her attention to the scenery. They were still in the low country, and around the coastal flats through which they were travelling she knew to expect coconut palms and later fields of paddy. She asked Roddy about it all, but found him disappointingly vague. Either that or his attention was on April.

Yet somehow he did not seem so absorbed with her sister as he had seemed before. He looked, or so Jane considered, almost introspective.

At her third attempt to inquire about the paddy fields, Joao Camoes, at a gesture, stopped the car.

'This is scandalous,' he said in mock-rebuke to his nephew, 'here we have a thirsty student and no spring of information at which to quench her thirst.'

Rodriguez mumbled something about never having found very much to interest him in the Sinhalese cultivation, a statement that brought a frown to his uncle and a quickly concealed quirk of amusement from April.

'We will change positions,' said Joao Camoes. 'You will sit where I am sitting, Rodriguez.'

He had got out as he spoke, and now stood impatiently waiting for Rodriguez to change seats. Once more the limousine set off.

Now Jane did not have to ask, she was told, and told so graphically that she found herself leaning forward in her seat to follow every gesticulation of the senhor, every wave to some new aspect.

'The flowers of the rice,' indicated Joao, 'are borne in a tuft, each on a separate stalk. The threshed paddy is sifted and winnowed clean and then separated into husked rice by hulling.'

'Are these crops,' asked Jane about the submerged fields, 'watered by rainfall or irrigation?'

'We are fortunate here in the more mountainous south with our monsoon rains from May to September, the lowland north is less rainy, so cannot depend, as we can, on natural methods.'

Now the car was beginning to climb, and with every

grade there was an almost startling change of scenery. Presently they came to a gigantic mass of rocks, and the driver stopped, evidently anticipating their interest. However, only Jane and Joao got out to admire the vista, Jane catching her breath at train lines set on mere shelves hewn from the scarped precipice.

'Why, yes,' said the senhor, surprised, 'there is a train, did you not know? We are quite proud of our comfortable and extremely scenic service.' Abruptly he left Jane staring out at ravines, crags and serrated edges to speak with the driver. Then he spoke with April and Rodriguez. Finally he came back to Jane.

'We are in luck, a train will be coming along fairly soon. It can take us some of the way to Ambanta. The car will await at an arranged station to pick us up again. You would like that?'

'Oh, senhor, yes, yes!' Jane's eyes were shining.

'I would like it myself,' he smiled, pleased at her eagerness, 'I am fond of trains.'

'All boys are.'

'Boys, senhorita?' He was laughing openly now.

'Men are only big boys.'

'I bow to the knowledgeable female.' He actually ... and laughingly ... did bow.

'But how,' he asked at once, 'do you explain my nephew Rodriguez who prefers to travel in the car?'

'I would explain that by saying that my sister prefers to remain as well,' proffered Jane.

'Love, senhorita?'

Jane knew that in April's instance ... just now, anyway ... the reason was comfort, April hated to move around more than she had to. However she did not correct the senhor.

'Perhaps,' she agreed. Then, to change the subject, 'But how can we take the train? There's no station.'

'It is well concealed behind that thicket of splendid

satinwood and mahogany, and its name, my man tells me, is Paraka.'

'Then,' said Jane gaily, 'by all means let us take the train from Paraka.'

She went back to the car to get her handbag and was rather surprised to receive from April instead of the glowering look she rather expected a listless one instead.

'Darling, you make me feel quite exhausted,' April mildly complained. 'You're actually going to walk to a funny little station and catch an odd little train. Well, it's your choice.' She leaned back against a nest of cushions that her Roddy thoughtfully had arranged.

Jane and the senhor set off down a narrow track and the big car resumed its journey again. Scarcely had it turned a bend in the road than the senhor asked rather abruptly, 'Your sister, Miss Jane, she was wholehearted, too?'

The 'Miss Jane' surprised Jane, but the question that came after her name surprised her more.

'Whole hearted, senhor?' she queried.

'You told me on the journey from Sydney that you had left nothing behind you, that you and your heart travelled together.'

'I and my heart,' concurred Jane.

'And Miss April? Pardon me if I sound probing, but she is – well—' He searched for a moment, then said with triumph: 'Preoccupied. Correct?'

'Yes. And I agree with you that she is just that. But I think it may be the heat.'

'When it is not hot? Not up here. Had you not noticed?'

Glad to be done with the rather edgy subject of April's moods, Jane acclaimed, 'Why, yes, it's hot no longer, it's quite pleasant.' She stopped abruptly, excited. 'Senhor, is that a monkey?'

'It is, child. It is a small variety called the macaque. The larger ones are called wanderoos, and they have black eyebrows, white beards and short hair.'

'But a monkey!' Jane beamed.

Joao shrugged tolerantly. 'Monkeys are everywhere in Ceylon except the settled areas.'

'What else could I meet?' Jane begged.

'It would be very unlikely that you would encounter an elephant, for they are, unfortunately, dying out in our dwindling jungles. I have, however, one at Ambanta that you will see.'

'Perhaps a leopard, senhor?'

'So near to the rest-house . . . yes, there will be a rest-house at the station . . . very improbable. But deer, perhaps, many wonderful birds, and, with extremely good fortune, a loris.'

'Loris?'

'A lemur about the size of a squirrel.'

'And why the extreme good fortune?'

'Because it is said that if you catch a tear from the eye of a loris you can make a love potion.'

'Is that,' asked Jane, 'another of the things in which you trade?'

'Love potions? No. But thank you, senhorita, for the idea. Look, we are through the track and at the rest-house. There is the small station, and if your eyes can see a long distance down to the grasslands you will glimpse a moving spot that is our train.'

Jane looked beyond the simple building and the small shelter to an aspect that fairly grabbed at her heart. Imposing cliffs, ribbed with rock, laced with tumbling waters, clad in unnumbered trees and knee-deep in flowers almost accosted her in their brilliant regalia.

'Joining the train at Paraka,' informed Joao Camoes, 'you will be spared Sensation Peak where the train crawls round a sheer ledge just wide enough to permit the track and where you can feel the wind blow. Even as it is, sen-horita, you will travel several curves where the guard and the driver can exchange civilities in passing. Have you a brave as well as a whole heart?'

'I will look only at the beauty,' she assured him back. She said it seriously, for she knew she had never known such beauty as this.

He nodded as gravely back again, then put his long, fine brown hands together as in a prayer and bowed very slightly. '*Ayubowen*,' he said.

'That is?'

'A greeting. A Sinhalese greeting to you for loving this lovely land.'

On an impulse Jane turned again to the vista, joined her own hands together and bowed. '*Ayubowen*,' she repeated.

When she turned back to the senhor it was to dark eyes so deep, so warm that for a moment she knew a strange yet curiously sweet trembling. In that moment their gazes met and held ... held until a small Sinhalese boy trotted up, proud in a white jacket over white shirt and sarong, to announce something to the senhor.

Joao nodded, then said a little diffidently to Jane, if this proud Portuguese knew diffidence, 'The rest-house has made tea. We have time before the train climbs the mountain.'

Suddenly shy herself, not understanding why, Jane followed the man and the boy to the verandaed building. There were several other small boys watching them from the shade of a golden bamboo, but obviously they were not as important as the small messenger, for their sarongs were just tubes of cotton, and they wore no shirts.

'Yes,' smiled the senhor, 'they envy our escort.'

'Class distinction in Ceylon?'

'Quite a lot, as a matter of fact. The "trousered" class is more esteemed than the saronged, and, of course, the takers of life, like hunters and fishermen, are what you might term on the outside.'

'Well,' smiled Jane, 'on the outside is the more pleasant in this rest-house.' She had glanced into the rather dim, through lack of sufficient windows, interior. 'Can we sit on the patio?'

'By all means.' Joao Camoes clapped his hands. He gave the order in Sinhalese, then turned to Jane.

'They will bring black tea which we will take with lime. Does that please you? I know that usually it is China tea that the English palate associates with the sliver of lemon, but you will like the tang, I am sure, of these local limes once they marry with the Souchong blend I have ordered.'

His choice of the word 'marry' reminded Jane of the advertising school award and how she had borrowed from the *Sinhalese Observer*. She laughingly told the senhor about it.

'Yes, it is true that in Sinhalese marriage the planets must be favourable, it is as important really as physical and mental compatability. Dowries, of course, are excluded.' He took out his cheroots. 'The Sinhalese husband,' he remarked, snipping off the top of the cigarillo, 'assumes the authority over his wife that was exerted by her father. The wife' – he lit the cheroot – 'defers in all ways to her lord.'

'Lord, senhor?'

'He is that – to her. She walks a few steps behind him, never sits in his presence or that of his friends.' A weave of blue smoke. Then: 'You wrote this exercise, senhorita, on a suggestion from an *Observer* that your sister had sent you?'

'Yes.'

'Why had your sister come alone to Ceylon?'

'Alone? She was on a ship.'

'You choose to misunderstand me.' The depth and

warmth had gone from the black eyes. 'I am well aware
that there would be many on the ship, that she would be
indeed surrounded, but that does not make for chaper-
onage, senhorita.'

Which is very important in Portugal, interpreted Jane,
and very important to you.

Aloud she said rather bluntly, 'She came by herself as
I came by myself.'

'But you came for a reason: to be with your sister. A
worthy reason, I think. But for what reason did your
sister come?'

Here could be a trap, recognized Jane. If she answered
back, as she felt dangerously like answering back: 'What
does it matter?' it could matter – for April. These things
mattered to him, to the senhor, and he could make them
matter for her sister.

It seemed a time for truth to Jane, so she answered the
truth. She told him of April's ambitions for the theatre.

'A singer?' he said, surprised. He smoked a while. 'Yet
she disembarked at Colombo.'

'She met Rodriguez.'

'He is not a singer.'

'I didn't say he was.'

'You misunderstand me again. How would my nephew
meet your sister?'

Exasperated, Jane burst out, 'How do young people
meet, senhor – have you forgotten?'

It was an unfortunate rejoinder, for she saw the red
mounting slowly from his throat, and knew he was very
angry.

'I do not know, senhorita, how young people meet in
your country, I only know how they meet in mine.'

'Dully.' She said it deliberately, for she was desperately
angry with herself and her clumsiness, and it made her
tongue acid.

He must have thought it acid, too, for after the tea and

116

lime had been left before them he looked long at the lime, then said, 'Cream would have been a blander choice.'

Jane did not reply. She knew that the Souchong and delicate sliver of fruit was very refreshing, but in her present state of emotions it almost choked her.

She was glad when he told her not to toy with her cup but drink the contents as the train was climbing the last rise.

She did so, then followed him to the small station just as the little puffing engine and its several carriages came to an exhausted halt.

He helped her into the one first-class compartment, then after a brief spell and some water the train set off.

It was quite as delightful . . . and hazardous . . . as Jane had anticipated. The British, the Portuguese said, had done this masterpiece of engineering, had thought out its ledges, its boring through mountains, its crossing of ravines, its climbing to dizzy heights. As for the beauty, the Pearl itself had supplied that.

On the rim of the tea district, at a tiny station very much like Paraka, Jane and Joao left the train and climbed a short track to the road. There, as Joao had planned, his car awaited. April sat in the car, but Rodriguez was standing some yards away talking to a man. Some yards away again was a shabby sports model whose London bus red hue brought instant recognition. It was Terry Marsden's. The man was Terry.

Jane half-stopped.

'What is it, senhorita?' It was Joao Camoes, cool, poised, waiting.

'That – that man—' she stammered.

'Yes. Mr. Marsden.'

'Why – why is he always—'

'Yes?'

'Nothing.' Again Jane had need to bite her lip.

'I think you are trying to ask why do you always seem

to encounter him. But that is understandable, surely? A journalist must be here, there, everywhere.'

'Even up in the Hills? The tea district?'

'We are not actually in the tea district yet, but yes, there, too. Possibly he is doing an article on the tea estates of Ceylon. There are not so many now, the days of the big resplendent holdings are gone, but there are many smaller acreages that are very lovely, and I think he might be doing a series for an English publication, who knows, even coming to Ambanta for copy, for our home, as you will see, senhorita, is very lovely.'

'You – you speak almost as though you approve of him, senhor.'

A look of surprise. 'But I do.'

'Yet on the night of my arrival—'

'That was entirely different.' The voice now was stiff. 'Any disapproval then was for you.'

'It sounded for him as well.'

'Then if it did it was because he was with you. As man to man I like the man. I know he is not regarded well in all walks, but I like him.'

'As man to man?' hazarded Jane.

'Exactly.'

'But when a woman is involved it's changed?'

'Yes. Is there anything unreasonable in that?'

She did not reply. She was too busy trying to decipher April's expression now that she had come near enough to read it. As before she found it not as easy as April was usually easy to read. All, indeed, she could say was that April was no longer listless.

Terry waved a casual arm to Jane, then went back to his rather vulgar model. Rodriguez held the door open, then he and Joao got in together, and they resumed their journey.

Rodriguez said, 'Terry Marsden is doing a tea series for an English syndicate. I said by all means to come to

Ambanta. That was right, sir?' April's brows met as they always did at her Roddy's deference.

'Perfectly right,' nodded Joao. He smiled perfunctorily at Jane. 'You see, I was correct.'

'How far have we to go now? I'm tired.' April added a plaintive tremor to her voice to hide the fretfulness.

But any fretfulness should have been wiped away the moment the car rounded the plantain-planted drive of the Hills home of Joao Camoes. As at the rest-house looking down on the splendid vista of the rock-ribbed, water-laced mountains, Jane's heart was grabbed up in the exquisite pain of the very beautiful once more.

The grass, greener than green, framing the splendid house ... no mere bungalow this ... the formal shrubs, the permitted intrusion of native flora, the Portuguese addition of stone benches, urns of spilling flowers, a fountain, a lily-pond, the profusion of terraces, summer houses and seat-encircled trees, reached at her. Surely the scene must reach April, too, even a little. At least take that unrest away.

But in the suite to which their bags were carried April might just as well have remained in the Sterne, before that in the Shangri-la. She went at once to the window to stare out ... but not, and Jane knew it, at the loveliness.

'That man—' she said, as Jane had said, but much more troublously. Strangely, inexplicably troublously.

'Well, what about him?' Jane asked practically. 'What does it matter that he's writing a series up here in the Hills? I mean, April, what can it matter to you?'

She expected a sharp retort, or a shrug of indifference, or a cutting criticism ... anything but what April *did* reply.

For:

'You don't understand!' April cried more than said. 'You don't see that I – that we—'

She wheeled sharply and went out of the room. The

next moment Jane heard her laughing in the hall with Rodriguez. But the laugh had a high unnatural note in it, it rang too gay.

Too gay, thought Jane, at a loss, for turquoise eyes that had slid away from hers to hide their tears.

April . . . April of all people *crying*!

CHAPTER SIX

By dinner that night April was entirely recovered. She had been taken on a tour of the house and grounds, and what had met her eyes had evidently settled a question. No longer she laughed over-gaily, slid her troubled glance away, her turquoise eyes were wide and bright, and she asked innumerable questions over the special Sinhalese meal that Joao had had his staff prepare.

As the staple Ceylon diet was rice, it was offered now in the form of *buriani*, made, the senhor said, from rice, mutton, ghee – which was buffalo milk butter – onions, cardamon and lemon-grass. A very hot *sambol*, made of chillies and lime juice, accompanied it, and a *pilau*, which was saffron rice with raisins and *cadju* – or cashew – nuts.

Jane, for her part, for the dishes were extremely satisfying, was glad that the sweets comprised only a dish of unusual ... for the visitors ... fruit, sour-sop, jaks, rambuttans, plantains from the trees that bordered the drive and pomegranates. As she peeled a plantain ... coarser than Australian bananas ... she let her glance rove round the large room, furnished entirely in cool rattan, but, because in these hills the air was more moderate, with the warm addition of fabric curtains instead of the coastal bamboo.

In the choice of drapes she saw the touch of the Portuguese, that trend to the heavy rather than to the airy, to rich, flowing brocades in glowing colours of clarets, russets, dark plums and dull golds.

Seeing her interest, Joao Camoes smiled, 'We had to have a touch of home. You see, this house was English-built, and though we love it, it was still not our own brain-child.'

'English-built? Yes, I can see that now.' Jane remembered wondering slightly upon arrival here at the faintly Tudor air. 'So the English came before the Portuguese.'

'On the contrary, senhorita, we were the first, in 1501. The date is carved on a rock which is now preserved in Colombo. But our particular family came after an English tea-grower, so, of course, the house was already built.' He smiled sincerely. 'I do not think we could have improved on it had it been the other way about.'

'It's a very beautiful place.' April was looking around her with charming enthusiasm. Only Jane, thought Jane, would glimpse the measured, the acquisitive look.

As though all at once she was unable to bide her time any longer, April asked with a sweet childish candour and naïveté of the senhor: 'Is it *your* house?'

'Mine.'

'Not Roddy's as well?'

'No, mine.'

With a deliberation that was so determinedly deliberate that every action seemed marked, seemed emphasized, the senhor took out his cheroots, adding, '*And* the firm, too, Miss Winthrop. *And* the tea estate.'

There was a little silence in the room. Jane felt herself stiffening – for April. Really, the senhor could have chosen a better time to tell her sister where she stood!

Then quite charmingly, very gallantly, Joao Camoes said, 'But Rodriguez is quite excellently placed. His jewels, I should say, are far worthier than mine.'

The little pulse that had begun to beat fiercely in April's fair brow at the news that Senhor Camoes had given her at once lost its fevered tempo.

'Roddy told me about his jewels,' she said eagerly. 'They – they are really his?'

'Very much so. Rodriguez always has taken far more

interest in that side of the business. He has an excellent collection of zircons, amethysts, topazes, moonstones.'

'Rubies and sapphires.' April barely breathed it. Her lips were parted in anticipation, her eyes dreamed.

Rodriguez, looking at her in positive enchantment, said softly, 'They are yours for the asking, I assure you of that.'

April smiled softly back at him, all radiance, all sweet young love.

'For myself,' the senhor remarked, though only Jane now listened, the other two were gazing at each other, 'my preference goes to a string of bean beads.'

He in his turn was looking at Jane, and, embarrassed, Jane came back with, 'Not an opal bracelet?'

'What is that?' he asked blandly. 'I have never seen one save on the wrist of your sister, Miss Winter.'

Still the other two remained unconscious of the interchange, so Jane, to break the tension, inquired busily, 'Where are these jewels found?'

'Ceylon's minerals are scattered in many districts, but we are fortunate enough to be able to mine in our own land. Ratnapura, into which the Ambanta property extends, is one of the most promising sources of this Isle of Gems, as it was once known. Sinbad' – he smiled at Jane – 'reputedly found many of his jewels here.'

'Is that true?'

'As true, I expect, as that Lanka—'

'Lanka?' she queried.

'Sri Lanka, meaning the resplendent land, and meaning Ceylon, was the original Garden of Eden, and as true as the belief that Solomon took his gold, silver, ivory, apes and peacocks from these very shores.

'For myself, as I said, it matters little. I prefer —'

'A bean necklace,' said Jane.

'With a firm cream throat to hang it on.'

'But I'm sallow,' Jane blurted. Suddenly sallow no

more but a flaming pink, she added, 'I mean – if you were speaking of me – I really mean—'

'I was,' he said clearly. 'And you are not.'

What she could have answered to that, Jane did not know. She was grateful that the interchange of looks between April and Rodriguez came to an end, that with the arrival of liqueurs the talk became general.

The girls went to bed early. Joao Camoes had planned a tea growing and packing inspection for the following day. He also wished to speak on business matters with Rodriguez.

'But do not feel you must go to your rooms on that account,' Joao bowed.

'We must,' laughed April. 'Well, I must, anyway. Beauty sleep, senhor.'

'That I can believe,' he said admiringly, and, indeed, April had never looked more beautiful. The talk of gems had animated her. Rodriguez's devotion had given her a radiance.

In the suite afterwards she was still in the same sweet mood.

'All those jewels, Jane,' she thrilled, 'and all of them dear Roddy's! You know how I've always felt over jewels. Roddy, too, is excellently placed, Joao said so himself. Undoubtedly the senhor has the greater wealth, but it would be tied up in this estate, and, darling, I'd be bored to tears. Besides, Roddy is fun, and' – a winsome glint – 'very easy to handle. Oh, yes, I think everything is fine.'

She even kissed Jane in her gay mood.

Yet, crossing to the window for a brief moment before she got into bed, the mood dropped from her like a discarded cloak, and she stood suddenly childish somehow. Vulnerable. Unsure.

There were no moods, even brief ones, the next day as Joao and Rodriguez showed the girls over the estate.

Even though April could barely sustain the interest she pretended, could barely wait for the inspection to be over so that she could see the jewels that Roddy had locked in the Ambanta strong-room and which he had promised to show to her, she was still sweet, gracious, and, outwardly anyway, enthralled.

It was not until Terry Marsden made an appearance that her veneer cracked . . . but that was hours away.

They set out after breakfast in two jeeps, April in her present mood going instinctively to Rodriguez's rover, leaving Jane perforce to climb into Joao's. It was a macadamized road for lorry transport, but very soon Joao, in the foremost jeep, turned into a 'cart-track', one of literally scores of such tracks, all steep of gradient, occasionally crossing bridges over ravines, over culverts, over 'Irish drains' which were paved crossings where the amount of water to be taken off did not justify the expense of more than just that.

The jeep went past storage for tools, storage for fertilizer, carpentry shops for the building of more and more dwelling houses, although there were many distributions already of small neat accommodation huts. They went past the nursery where the young tea plants waited, past Tamil boys working on boundary fences to keep out stray cattle and buffaloes. Everything, Jane noted, was done with almost mathematical accuracy, and this, Joao told her, was the pattern of the tea estates.

'Some "contour",' he said, 'some "slope", but always we work by compass and line.'

Close planting, Jane found when they reached the first work section, was practised, enough breathing space for the tea bushes to grow to their full stature, but not too much, for they were also expected to provide an umbrella for the soil.

'In my matured fields,' said Joao, 'I do not like to see any ground. Not' – a little sadly – 'that even green umbrellas in rhythmical rows can bring back one small iota of the natural beauty that once was.'

They proceeded along to the plucking, and here even April did not have to pretend enchantment. It was like looking at gay butterflies fluttering above green grass to see the pluckers working their way along the rows. They carried large bamboo baskets slung to their backs by means of a cord wound round their foreheads, and as most of the pluckers were young, pretty women whose taste ran to vivid colours, the rows of green tea bushes were interspersed with brilliant reds, purples and golds.

The bushes themselves, trained to a height of three feet by pruning, yielded a crop every two weeks. This 'flush', or crop, demonstrated Joao, comprised of a tender closed leaf bud and the next two leaves, young and succulent. They alone were plucked. It was fascinating to watch the women's fingers darting over the surface of each bush, gathering the crop in small heaps, then throwing them over the shoulder into the waiting basket. The leaf was not to be crushed, not to be bruised, and Jane marvelled that with all the speed this was never done to the tender plants.

The leaf next was weighed on the field and then transported to the factory. There it went through five processes that took the party the entire morning to examine . . . the withering, rolling, fermenting, firing and finally grading.

Jane, standing at last beside a fragrant heap of black, crisp tea, waiting for sorting, sifting then packing, said thirstily that that was all she could now ask: a cup of green umbrellas reduced to an amber beverage.

'And you shall have it,' Joao assured her.

He was in a happy mood, as elated over his tea as April had been over Rodriguez's gems last night.

April smiled brightly but a little pityingly at his enthusiasm. Jane knew her sister was thinking that it had all been very interesting – if you liked that sort of stuff.

Sipping the tea that Joao had ordered to be served in the overseer's office, April's full mouth kept up its happy quirk. She was thinking of pigeon's blood rubies, no doubt, thought Jane tolerantly, grateful that at least April could smile, could forget her moods.

Then the curve was going quickly downward. The mood was returning. Returning with Terry Marsden strolling casually into the office, greeting everyone yet no one, giving April a long cool stare, seating himself without being invited, helping himself to tea, taking out his notebook.

'I'd like your opinion,' he was saying in a clear arresting voice to Senhor Camoes, 'as to deep forking. Heresy? A waste of good top-soil? What method do you use' – he paused – 'your Excellency?'

He had chosen his moment. The question, intelligent, to the point, had silenced the tea-drinkers so that Terry's voice cut knife-sharp into the quiet.

The effect was almost electric, even to Jane, who had been told of the senhor's rank before. She had neither believed, nor disbelieved, it. She had not been really very interested. But April . . .

April's cheeks were drained, her eyes were so big they seemed to use nearly all her face. She looked from Terry to Joao, then back to Terry again.

Into the silence came Terry's voice once more. 'That's true.' The Englishman grinned.

There was another silence, a silence fairly screaming out to be broken, broken by a denial . . . or an agreement. An agreement it was.

Completely bored, quite indifferent, Joao Camoes tossed, 'Quite true. I am the Conde de Camoes. Your question again, Marsden? Oh, yes, deep forking, was it not? In my opinion, and on my estate—'

Jane did not hear the rest. Her attention was on April, April rising slowly, almost, it seemed, with difficulty, from her chair, crossing to stand at the door to look out. She did not turn back until, the deep forking question settled, Joao Camoes issued an invitation to Terry Marsden to move into Ambanta and finish his series there.

'We have ample room. You can have the quiet that writing demands.'

'But your other guests—' Terry demurred falsely, for his eyes were gleaming wickedly – glinting at April.

What else could April do than murmur a politeness? Jane smiled at Terry, to which he responded with a sly wink.

On the way back to the big house Jane found herself in the showy red sports car. Marsden quite impudently had placed her there, but, apart from a momentary stiffening of the straight back, a brief disapproving line to the long mouth, the senhor paid little attention. Even if he had wished to keep the previous arrangement, he had no opportunity to do so. Making some excuse, April got in beside Joao, leaving Rodriguez to travel back alone.

Starting the noisy engine of the London bus red car, Terry smiled sourly.

'She's wasting no time,' he said.

'What do you mean, Terry?'

They were on the cart track now, Terry keeping within seeing distance of the jeeps for the connecting tracks wound intricately and it would have been easy to get lost.

'Oh, come off it, Jane, you know what I mean. You saw milady's face just now.'

'When you – when you—'

'Spilled the news of the peerage? Yes. You could see change of mind flicker across that lovely face just as unmistakably as if it was written down in words of one syllable. Two syllables really.' He laughed harshly. When Jane did not inquire, he said, 'Count-ess.' With emphasis on the 'ess.'

'Oh, Terry!' she exclaimed reproachfully.

'But it's true, isn't it?'

'Not true.' Jane spoke determinedly. 'She's going to look at Rodriguez's jewel collection this afternoon.'

'Betcha!' Terry inserted almost brutally.

'I beg your pardon?'

'I bet you the title wins over the rubies.'

Jane did not reply. The title would win – when it was April. How could it not win? She wanted to feel indignant against her sister, but all at once, she could not have said why, she felt inexpressibly sad. For herself.

'Terry,' she asked presently, 'why did you do it?'

'Had to, Janey.' His words were a little thick.

'Had to?' Jane could not understand.

In a staccato voice now Terry tossed, '. . . When . . . if . . . I mean if pigs fly . . . you understand . . . well, I'd want to have everything levelled out.'

'I don't know what you're talking about, Terry.'

Marsden said with an attempt of lightness, 'That makes two of us.'

As they came down the drive of plantains he asked Jane what she would be doing that afternoon.

'I told you.' Jane was cross. 'April will be inspecting the jewels.'

'Not unless Joao inspects them, too. Anyway, I never asked about milady, I asked about you.'

'And why? It won't matter to you. You'll be writing in some quiet corner.'

'Not me. It was good of Camoes to invite me, and I rushed the invitation, but I'm a newspaperman and I need no quiet corner, my love.'

'Don't call me that.'

'Why not, Jane? Is it because you are someone else's love?' His eyes probed hers.

She did not answer. She just stared steadily . . . and

candidly, or so she thought ... back at him. She was surprised, and a little dismayed, when presently he said softly, 'Poor kiddo, poor little Jane.'

'What, Terry?'

He did not explain, and in some odd way she was relieved for that. She got out of the sports car, did not wait to hear his proposal for the afternoon but hurried along to her room.

The moment she entered the room, which adjoined April's by a communicating door, her heart sank. April was standing in the middle of the room, no dreaming by the window now, and she was furious.

'That Marsden has edged himself right in this time. Of all the insufferable louts!'

She paced the room, then said, not quite so angrily, 'And yet in a way he's done me a service. I didn't know ... I never dreamed ...'

'You mean,' said Jane flatly, 'the Senhor Camoes being a Count.'

A word of two syllables, she thought, Count-ess. Count-ess.

'Of course,' April said.

'It makes a difference?'

'Darling, don't be completely naïve. Money will buy Roddy's rubies and sapphires, but money will never buy Joao's title. The Countess. *The Condesa.*' Quite unashamedly April thrilled.

'But he doesn't use it. Joao doesn't go by his title.'

'Not now, but when he's married it could be a different tale.'

'It would be redundant at Ambanta, and he loves and intends to stop at Ambanta.'

'That also could be a different tale. Oh, if only I'd known all this before I wouldn't have wasted the time that I have.'

'You mean—'

'Yes, my little greenhorn, I mean just that. Don't look so righteous. Wouldn't you?'

'No.'

'If you had known Joao was a count?'

'I did know. At least' – at a sudden narrowing of April's turquoise eyes – 'I'd heard Terry mention it.'

'Oh, so that's it! That's why you haven't left any stone unturned to worm your own way into Joao's attention. That's why you stopped back with him at the restaurant after the dance fiesta, travelled in the train with him, rushed to be in his jeep this morning, asked questions aimed to alert him as to your intelligence, for it would have to be intelligence, wouldn't it, Jane? You certainly have nothing else!'

'April!'

'You little brown nothing, how dare you pit yourself against me. Oh, yes, you did. Deliberately you withheld his title from me, for you saw yourself in the role of countess. You! Plain Jane! That's a laugh.' But April did not laugh.

'You nearly fell over yourself telling me how Roddy was well-placed, you wanted a match with Roddy and me so that you – that you—'

'*April!*'

This time Jane's voice did reach her sister, and the lovely girl stopped her pacing to come and stand by Jane.

'I'm sorry.' Typical of April, she could subside at once. 'None of it's true, you probably are the greenhorn that I said, the fact that Joao is a count would mean nothing to you. I should have remembered how you always were a rather sweet imbecile, Janey. Take it all as unsaid. I don't know what's come over me. I always was an acid drop, but never as acid as this.'

'Does all this mean that you're not – will not—'

'No, it doesn't, if you're referring to my plans – with Count Camoes.' April lit a cigarette then exhaled slowly.

'They go right ahead. I start this afternoon, Jane. When Joao spoke on the way back about his wretched elephant I immediately clamoured to see it ... implied that cold things like rubies were nothing to a big clumsy beast.' Only I said something like the noble jungle king.' She laughed.

'No doubt,' she resumed harshly, 'Roddy will be desolated. I only hope he doesn't take it out on the jewels and fling them away. Not that it matters to me, I'll never wear them. Though I've been thinking ...' She stood there absorbed in her thoughts.

Then she turned to Jane and said without a trace of embarrassment, 'I've been thinking about tiaras, Jane, and whether a Portuguese Countess. ...'

CHAPTER SEVEN

As it turned out four, not two, went to see the Ambanta elephant that afternoon, April, Joao, Jane and Terry. Rodriguez either had other business to attend or was sulking because of the treatment he was receiving. When Jane spoke to him at lunch she saw some sulkiness but much more conjecture. The rather boyish glance every time it was turned on April held an almost estimating glint.

April had put on perfectly tailored jodphurs for the inspection that Jane had not seen before. Beside them her own slacks looked shabby, and, no doubt through wear, rather baggy. But April was pleased with her sister's appearance, seeing it in contrast to her own, and forgave Jane for being included in the party.

She did not forgive Terry, though. After giving him a sharp loathing look when he joined them on the veranda she never intentionally glanced his way again.

Joao took the lead through the bushes and the others followed in file, April behind Joao, Terry at the rear. The elephant, Joao related as they clambered down the gully reserved for Vasco ... the Ambanta elephant had been given a Portuguese name ... was not a ferocious king of beasts. 'I must beg your pardon,' he paused to turn to say to the girls, 'but the elephant has always been that to me, and not the lion. No, on the contrary he is entirely vegetarian. He eats wood pulp from tree branches.'

April said naïvely she was pleased about that.

'Yes, you would make a tender dinner,' smiled Joao. Terry's wicked eye caught Jane's and ticked up a point for Jane's sister.

'Wild elephants are still around,' related Joao, 'but when I say wild I do not mean savage, for elephants are seldom that. There are "rogues" ... we have one on the rim of the grassland worrying us now ... but it is an exception, never a rule.'

'How did Vasco come to Ambanta?' called Terry.

Joao smiled. 'He simply came. In all the animal world there is always a certain one, an "Elsa", shall we say? who needs more than a fellow beast, who needs man. Vasco just came, as I said, came, I really believe, for love.

'We never fenced him ... we left the way open for him to return to his haunts, but the years went on and he stopped. So' – Joao shrugged – 'this became his gully and we did enclose it. Fortunately there are many trees thus a lot of wood pulp, for our Vasco has a large capacity.'

They were almost at the bottom of the gully now and Jane called out that she could hear water.

'Then we are lucky. I hoped we would be. Vasco will be bathing. Elephants bathe very regularly, they are quite Roman in their allegiance to the bath, but Vasco is almost an addict. It is an extremely pleasant sight to see an elephant enjoying his bath. I'm sure you will enjoy it as I do.'

'Have you really made a bath for him?' asked April facetiously. Fecklessness suited her, made of her a winsome little girl.

'We have blocked up a stream,' smiled Joao, 'big enough for Vasco's outsize. Hush!'

But there was no need for any hushing. The wallowing, snorting, trumpeting and rolling could not have been missed even if one wanted to miss it. Turning a bend of the rough track, they came in full view of the elephant cleansing, relaxing and having fun all in the one go. It was delightful to watch, and Jane laughed aloud in her pleasure. April did, too, but from farther back. She did not want splashes on the silk shirt she had tucked into the new jodphurs.

'Our elephants are smaller than Indian and African, and the tuskers are not very prevalent. Vasco is a tusker, though in India and Africa such minor tusks would be scorned. I have seen some tuskers also among the wild ones.'

Vasco began rolling, playful as a puppy, but when he got up, forefeet first, then his hind feet, any likeness to a puppy was dispersed, he was a veritable mountain of beast, a great grey dome, even though, being Sinhalese, he was a smaller breed.

He came up to the party, allowing Joao to fondle him. Then he looked at the girls.

'He would like to pick you up,' invited Joao. 'I assure you that once you get used to it there is nothing like an elephant ride. It is a quite superb sensation being borne as high as the topmost leaves of the tree.'

April had shrunk back, so not to embarrass her ... also with a thought to what she might say later ... Jane refused, too.

Disappointed, Joao said, 'I am so heavy for this small one.' None the less he submitted, and the 'small one' took him up with ease and put him on his back.

At that moment there was a bellow that froze the girls and Terry to the ground where they stood. It came from the bottom of the gully, and there was no mistaking the sound. It was the same noise that Vasco had made, but this time it was angry, raging.

As if propelled by automation Joao slid from Vasco's back, calling at the same time for Marsden to retreat with April and Jane.

'I told the Tamils to see to the boundary at the gully bottom,' Joao was calling as he backed the unwilling Vasco. 'They must have forgotten — either that or the beast down there in his raving has broken the fence.'

A moment later there was no beast down there, it was literally upon Vasco, upon the four of them, for the party found it much harder to climb up than clamber down, and April at the rear, or rather the front now in the retreat, in her frantic fear was making little progress, slipping back as fast as she strained up, delaying the rest.

With an oath Joao pushed past to her and pulled her up into his arms.

'Move. *Move!*'

Taking his cue, Terry did the same with Jane. An enraged bellowing stopped them. Whether still in danger, or not, they simply had to turn and see.

The wild, or 'rogue' elephant . . . a tusked one . . . was raging down on Vasco, his small eyes like fire. They stood in horror as his great shape crashed out at the Ambanta elephant, his tusks gleaming in the slats of sun forcing their way through the thick leaves of the trees like white flames. He was seeking to sink the tusks into Vasco, but Vasco had other ideas. With unbelievable manoeuvrability for a huge grey dome he stepped back, then as the rogue having misjudged slipped past him he did some tusk work of his own.

Now the bellowing fairly shook the jungle, but, tasting his own medicine, the invader must have decided he had had enough, for he turned and fled. Vasco chased him, then as they all still stood wordless, looking at each other, came lumbering back again. He sidled to Joao to repeat his tricks, but instead Joao cut down some green wood and gave it to him.

'I think,' he said, 'we've had enough, old fellow, today.'

'What will you do about that other dreadful beast?' asked April when they reached the top once more. 'Send someone out to shoot it?'

'It would be rather difficult, it could be far into the grasslands by this time. No, there has been too much elephant slaughter already. No doubt the so-called rogue has suffered some wound, and in his blind pain has been momentarily mad. As I said before, mostly they are easy beasts.'

'Easy for Joao to say that, I'm sure,' April grumbled as the girls changed for dinner. 'How could you stand down there looking as though you enjoyed yourself, Jane?'

'I did . . . until the incident occurred.'

'I didn't at any time. I hated it. I hate the great outdoors.'

'Then, April—'

'Don't say it, Jane. I have my own foolproof solution. I think you know what I mean.'

'Back to Portugal?'

'England, France.' April took a long deep breath. 'The world. With Joao's money and with Joao's title there's no limit, no limit at all.'

Then . . . to Jane's idea quite inconsequentially, with no pertinent reference at all . . . April added: 'Let Marsden write an article on that.'

At dinner that night April again was to suffer a shock. Last night it had been the shock of the announcement, by Joao Camoes, that it was the Camoes money and not the Carreras, the Camoes tea estate and the Camoes exporting trade.

The jewel talk had softened the blow, and the shock had become a turning point. But now, with the turn made again, the turn currently to the count and not his nephew, a nephew evidently well out of the running on his own accord as well as April's, to judge by Rodriguez's more enlightened than disillusioned look, a barrier and a possible hitch cropped up when Joao Camoes, the coffee having arrived, leaned intentionally over and said to April, 'So you are a singer.'

There was no opportunity to dart Jane a quick and inquiring glance, so April marked time by saying sweetly, 'More or less.'

'More or less? But you were on your way to further your career.'

Whether to agree, or protest, to be ambitious or to shrink from possible success. For really the first time in her life, Jane thought, she watched her sister and saw indecision. She wanted desperately to help her. It was no use, she knew wretchedly, one can't arrange one's heart, and I'm really fond of April.

'She sings beautifully,' she put in proudly.

'And yet,' frowned the senhor as he had frowned before, 'she stops her journey at our island where there is no opening for a singer at all.'

There were a few moments of silence round the table. Rodriguez's attention was on his cup. Jane was waiting for April's move. Joao was reaching for his eternal cheroots. Terry Marsden was leaning back, his lips twisted in a wry grin. Why, he's enjoying himself, Jane thought.

April's face was a study. She was no fool, she had perceived by this what value a Portuguese puts on social behaviour, especially social behaviour in a young unmarried girl. As an Australian she might call it stuffy, but as an Australian with an eye for another nationality, for – yes, she admitted it to herself, and to Jane – a title, she would forgive the stuffiness. Now that she had made her final decision she could not offer the romantic excuse of Rodriguez, of her eyes encountering his, and after that ... after that ...

No, most certainly that would not do.

What then? *What?* She had lost her money, so had to get off the ship? She had been in indifferent health and had decided not to go on?

No, money could be replaced, at least as far as the senhor knew, for she never had told him of their straitened circumstances, it could be replenished, and as for her health, it obviously was, and had been, good. Besides, everyone knew that these days the medical attention on ships was as excellent as on shore. What then? What?

All at once it came to April. She knew. Hanging her head a little, biting her lip, she managed a small crystal tear, just, Jane remembered, as she had been able to manage tears when she was young and wanted something that she could not have. But, Jane remembered hollowly now, finally got.

'What is it, child?' The senhor had got up from the table to cross to April. 'Child,' he said gently, 'you are distressed.'

'I – I never wanted to come. I—' There was a pause, a long tremulous pause. 'I never wanted to sing.'

'You . . . but I don't understand. What is this?'

In a voice so soft that it could barely be heard April whispered lies that Jane could not really believe she was listening to with her own ears. How all her life dear Mummy – yes, she was that for all that she was an ambitious mother – and darling Jane, who always asserted that the next best thing to success was to be a sister to success, had pushed April.

'Because' – now April lifted the turquoise eyes with the crystal glint of tears in them – 'because you see, Joao, I really had such a little voice. Such a very unimportant, such a small voice. That, anyway, was obvious to me. A voice only destined to – to—'

'Sing lullabies?' It was Terry Marsden, his lips twisted in the old derisive grin.

'Marsden!' It was the senhor.

'Sorry, Joao. Sorry, milady.'

'*Marsden!*'

'I beg your pardon, Miss Winthrop, do please proceed.'

'I suppose I could have held out, should have held out, but – but I loved them, Joao, and they had sacrificed a lot for me. Lessons, you understand, and then finally the money for this journey. But – but I found I couldn't last out, that I couldn't go through with it, so — so when the ship reached Colombo, I — I just got off.'

'And your sister, Miss Jane Winter, instead of coming, as I understood, to join you, to chaperone you, came instead to urge you to go on?'

April's 'Yes' was so low and so troubled it barely could be heard at all.

Presently Joao turned to Jane, just as she had known he would. But though she had known, she had still not prepared an answer to the question she knew he would ask.

'Is this true, Miss Jane?'

Jane sat very still. What was the use now of speaking the truth? she thought miserably. It would do her no good and it would do April harm.

'I suppose,' she evaded, 'it is more or less like that.'

'Like what?'

'Like you just said.'

'And like your sister said?'

'More or less.'

'If that is meant for a clever evasion I do not find it so.'

'It was just meant as a reply. Really, senhor, aren't you making a great deal out of nothing? A mountain from a molehill? It is, after all, of no importance at all.'

'No importance?' He stood quite furiously above Jane, and for some reason in his grey suit Jane thought of the height and bulk of the grey dome down in the jungle gully. Joao's king of beasts.

'No importance!' said this king ... no, Jane thought a trifle hysterically, this *count*. 'I consider it of vast importance. In fact I am very concerned over this what you call small affair. To force a person ... or should I say oblige a person ... to do what they do not want to do is little short of criminal. How much have I seen of it in my own country? An estate handed to a first son whose interests were in medicine, in engineering, in anything but the cork and lime groves. And then the second son, with his heart fairly crying out for the soil, sent to some business house instead.

'My own sister did it with Rodriguez. Nothing would please her than that he come out here, where obviously he is not at home.'

Rodriguez glanced up, but only just that. He looked down on his cup again.

'He was born for an *avenida*,' went on Joao, 'an avenue, for urban activities. Is that not so, my boy?'

'It is true,' admitted Rodriguez. 'All I ask is my car to run up to the mountains, to run down to the coast, to run into the city. The usual pleasant things a civilized place bestows. This Ceylon . . .' He got restlessly up and went to the window.

'You see,' said Joao, 'he is not happy and never has been. That is why . . .' He looked down on April's lovely flaming hair but, discreetly, did not finish his words.

'You will understand then, Miss Winter, why I have "exaggerated". I was very angry with my sister for her lack of intuition.'

'Then,' said Jane coldly, 'why did you not fight it, refuse to accept Rodriguez?'

'She was my senior.' He was as cold as Jane.

'But you,' she came back, 'were male.'

Terry Marsden chose to intervene then, and his intervention brought April's head up again, her eyes dark with hate for the journalist.

'All very interesting,' Terry yawned, 'but the proof of the pudding, as they say, is in the eating.'

'What do you mean, Marsden?'

'Shouldn't we judge by letting the lady sing?'

'I don't wish to sing,' April said with a little shiver.

Terry said deliberately, 'No, I bet you don't.'

'I do not follow,' said the senhor. 'If Miss Winthrop is

too upset to sing then of course she must not sing.'

'And we must all believe her story since we cannot hear her, her story that she has not, as she insists, any voice. And' – flicking a glance at Jane – 'disbelieve her sister.'

That was a poser for the senhor. He studied his cheroot for a moment, then said very gently to April, 'You could perhaps sing a small song to satisfy our cynical visitor?'

Terry, undismayed by the tag, simply sat on and grinned.

'Of course I'll sing,' agreed April docilely. 'You must understand, Joao, that actually I love to sing. It's just that I'm not, and never will be, what has been put upon me. And that is a real singer. A singer in the true meaning of the word.'

Terry put in, 'Can *we* judge that?'

'By all means, but' – triumphantly – 'I only sing to an accompaniment.'

'I can accompany you,' said Terry. 'These ink-stained fingers can rattle a scale as well as write poems.'

'A scale!' April shuddered. She added – softly for Terry – 'A poem! You?'

He shrugged, untouched, and April went on aloud more triumphantly again, 'There's no piano.'

'Ah, but there is.' It was Joao now. 'In the other wing. Quite a good one, I have been told by visitors who are musically inclined. If you have finished your coffee, ladies, shall we proceed there now. That is' – with solicitude to April – 'if all this is not too presumptive, too much of a burden, an imposition, dear child.'

The dear child smiled up at him, a rather wobbly, pathetic, tremulous smile, and said, 'I'll try. But you know what to expect.'

'I'm sure it will be charming.'

'If uneventful?'

'I do not ask for an event.'

'Thank you, senhor.'

They walked to the other wing, where the senhor called for drinks, and while they talked desultorily April looked through some music that Rodriguez had found. The young man was more friendly now, his resentment was gone, he was looking upon April as another ill-cast performer in life, a fellow sufferer, in fact.

April found a song that Jane had never heard her sing before, in fact had never heard at all.

'This.' She handed it to Terry. 'Is it too difficult for you?'

'I can promise you a note here and there.'

'That will be enough.' She gave him a brittle smile.

But Terry played more than a note here and there. He played fluently, quite excellently, with feeling. Jane, recalling how April had at least been genuinely carried away with music, though whether the carrying away had been artistic or not she never had had the art herself to judge, wondered how April would be able to resist putting everything into the song she had chosen.

For putting nothing was what April planned, Jane felt sure of that. She would have to prove to the Senhor Camoes that small, unimportant, trivial voice. And, cleverly, cunningly, with little brow-creasing pauses here and there, difficulties, wrong notes, wrong timing, convincing passages of music now and then to vindicate to a small extent her mother's and her sister's selfish attitude, sufficiently, anyway, not to make a fabrication of it all, she stumbled, smiled, started again, finally got through the song.

That it was an ordeal was evident by the carnation pink patches on her fair skin. Again the turquoise eyes glinted with tears. She looked lost, troubled, infinitely sweet. An appealing child.

Rodriguez fussed around her, said comfortingly that she had done very well, that really it was a very nice voice.

The senhor said softly, gently, 'Now I understand.'

But Terry Marsden, back from the piano stool now, downing the brandy that had been brought for him while he accompanied April in one vicious gulp, said ... but only Jane could hear: 'You lying, you damn lying girl!'

Once she had made her decision April proceeded on her chosen path without pause or deviation. There was something quite unnatural and ruthless in the single-minded way she went about achieving her goal.

Even for April it was a little too much April, Jane thought, dismayed. Her half-sister had always been a selfish girl, but there had been chinks in her armour. Now there were no chinks. She was completely encased in a hard, impenetrable shell. Hard – for everyone save Joao Camoes.

There had been a few words between the girls on the night of the piano incident, but they had been brief and to the point – and mainly April's.

'I'm sorry about the showdown this evening, Jane, but in a way you have only yourself to blame. You should never have spoken to Joao about my voice. I had no alternative other than to do what I did.'

'Make ambitious pushers of Mother and me?'

'You're over-sensitive. I wasn't that hard, I simply implied that you both saw in me what was not really there.'

'Isn't it there, April?'

'A voice? Oh, one of a sort.'

'But not the sort you used for Senhor Camoes.'

'The Conde de Camoes, Jane, and there is your answer. *Count* Camoes.'

April had wheeled round and gone to her own room, indicating that the matter was closed.

As regarded the senhor, of course, it was only just opened. The following morning April began what Terry

Marsden impudently tagged ... to Jane ... the Peerage Pursuit. At times more impudently still: the Royalty Race. Without the shade of a doubt the pursuit, or the race, went very well; the senhor was kindness and solicitude itself to April. Sometimes it seemed that April had only to ask and it was given ... but if she asked for the removal of Terry Marsden, which Jane considered likely, that was one thing that was not given. The newspaperman stayed on.

That it infuriated April was evident very often to Jane, when, in the safety of their suite, April had need no longer to contain herself.

'That man ... that wretched man, why does he stay on?'

'It's his work, April, he's doing this series for an English syndicate.'

'So he says! Look, Jane, you're interested in writing yourself, can't you get in with him and see whether he's really doing these articles or imposing on our hospitality.' – *Our*, noted Jane.

'I'm quite sure he's here to write,' defended Jane.

'And I'm quite sure he's not.'

'Then what?'

'He's here to – to—' But April could not, or would not, finish.

'I loathe him,' was all she said.

Out of fellow interest Jane did speak with Terry, and found, as she had said to her sister, that he indeed was writing a series of articles.

'So milady had her doubts, did she?' grinned Terry maliciously. 'What does she think I live on, young Jane?'

'Just now she thinks you're living on her hospitality.'

'Her?' Terry was nothing if not quick.

'Actually April said "our",' Jane admitted.

'Of course. And now she's anxious to be rid of me. Right?'

'Well—'

'Don't hedge, little one, I'm tough.'

'Then – yes.'

'Good for her and bad for me. But the Count wants me here, so good for me and bad for her. And keeping in mind that as in Ceylon as well, the Portuguese male has the first and last word, I think we can say with assurance that the newspaperman stays on.'

'Has he?' asked Jane with interest. 'Does the Portuguese male—'

She stopped, embarrassed. Terry, always restless, always moving somewhere else, had left her, and unnoticed, Joao Camoes had appeared.

'Senhorita?' he asked, brows raising. 'You were saying?'

'I was saying it to Mr. Marsden, senhor.'

'But surely, being a Portuguese subject, a Portuguese can answer more fully. You began "Does the Portuguese male—"'

It was simply no use trying to evade this man. How many times had Jane tried it before?

She said, with the hint of a sigh, 'Does the Portuguese male, like his Sinhalese counterpart, have complete authority?'

'You mean over his female partner?'

'Yes.' Now Jane's cheeks were flaming. Why did she always have to flush like this?

She awaited his lofty reply, his arrogant assurance that most certainly the Portuguese male held the reins. So much so did she anticipate the answer that when Joao Camoes spoke, said what he did, it came as a shock. For quietly, almost tentatively, the big man said: 'We like to think, Miss Jane, that we meet half-way.'

A surprising but very comfortable position . . . for both sides . . . had become established between April and Rodriguez.

Since the night of April's poor little performance a kind of *esprit de corps* had risen between them, the fellow feeling of misdirected lives, on one hand the subjected singer, on the other the obligatory alien. They exchanged little sighs of unwilling concession, little moues of unhappy resignation, and both obviously preferred their new relationship.

'He's quite a nice lad,' April said to Jane . . and Jane smiled secretly. It seemed impossible that only several weeks ago her sister had declared she loved the young man. But that, of course, had been before she had known that Joao was Count Camoes.

The very thought of the senhor being a count intoxicated April, but not so much that she did not pursue her course soberly and with meticulous care. She became more out-of-doors, accompanied Joao on estate inspections, spent a day with him in one of the tea tallying rooms, drove with him in the jeep to see to the boundary fences, when she knew he would be coming out on the patio for an evening smoke bribing a Tamil boy to drive her past the bungalow in a cart, the while she sat gaily at the boy's side laughing irresistibly like a bright young schoolgirl.

That he was amused by it all was evident by his gay rejoinders, his frequent smiles as though he was inwardly as well as outwardly entertained.

April even nerved herself to be picked up down the elephant gully by Vasco, and, knowing April, surely there was no deeper sacrifice, Jane thought, on any woman's part. But when Joao proposed . . . no, not proposed, *arranged*, for the Portuguese senhor, in spite of that assertion that the Portuguese male and female met half-way, still, in Jane's opinion, more often decreed than agreed

... that the house-party make a pilgrimage to Adam's Peak, for the first time April quailed.

She had been told all about Sri Pada ... the Sacred Footprint ... and how the eight-mile ascent which was literally an eight-mile staircase was enough to tire a healthy athlete let alone ... let alone ...

In the privacy of their rooms April shuddered.

'I can't. I can't! Why isn't the wretched Peak up in the north of Ceylon and not so horribly handy to here?'

'It can't be so bad, many of the Buddhists carry their children or support their ailing relatives up the trail. It's the attitude to it that counts, April. It's not to be approached as just another peak to be conquered, but a pilgrimage.'

'Well, let the pilgrims do it. I'm not one.'

'Then tell Joao. I'm sure he'll understand.'

'Oh, Jane, don't be naïve!'

April toyed with a dozen excuses. Health? No. Just now she was sure that the Count ... she always called him the Count ... was quite delighted with her sturdiness. How many times had he said that she deceived her fragile look. A strained ankle? No, he was so meticulous he undoubtedly would summon a physician and have the foot examined.

Perhaps she could suddenly find the prospect of the emotional side of the Sacred Footprint a little too disturbing for her delicate senses. No, that would not do. Joao had commended her practicality.

There seemed no way out but to suffer, and to April eight miles was a lot of suffering. Then, with typical April-luck, April escaped. It happened on the very morning of the expedition, April even dressed for the adventure, so that no one, not even Jane, could doubt April's integrity.

Rodriguez was taken ill. The doctor who attended the neighbouring tea estates was summoned and diagnosed a mild food poisoning, then traced the source. He said that most certainly Rodriguez must stay at home, that any other members of the household who had eaten of the particular suspect spice should take a similar precaution, for even though they had no ill effects as yet, it could be very uncomfortable for them once on the steep track.

It was literally manna from heaven for April. With a stricken expression she clapped her hand over her mouth and called, 'I ate that dish!'

Hardly were the words out of her mouth than Terry Marsden called, 'I ate it, too.'

'Three out of a party of five,' demurred Joao, 'makes it no party at all. I think we must call off the expedition till later.'

April, restraining herself with difficulty from flicking Terry a furious look, changed the look to quick appeal ... to Jane.

Jane knew that even though April did not want her sister to be with Joao, she still wanted Jane to clamour to go, and so cancel the Adam's Peak expedition as far as April was concerned. And why not? thought Jane. The anticipation of the Peak had enthralled her right from the first. She had read all about the ringing of the bell at the entrance of the temple, once for every time a pilgrim had climbed Sri Pada, and she yearned to begin to ring.

The longing must have shown in her, for she became aware that the senhor was looking at her with understanding.

'You are disappointed, child?'

'Yes. But it doesn't matter.'

'It does. And you will not be disappointed. We will leave these too-greedy children and go to Sri Pada ourselves.'

Now April, for all her meaning looks, was not so pleased, but there was nothing she could do about it.

Either the party was cancelled for today and they all went later on or Jane and Joao went and April escaped the ordeal she dreaded. She decided the latter the better of the two evils, and followed Jane and Joao out to the car that Joao would drive himself over the ranges, Rodriguez remaining listlessly on the patio, Terry sauntering rather jauntily behind the girls and Joao, to call to the adventurers to be very careful, darlings, and please, dear Jane, to take great notice so that she could be told everything, every beautiful detail of Sri Pada which, unhappily, she was to miss.

At that Terry gave an impudent grin.

The car skimmed down through the drive of plantains then turned north-west into terrain that Jane had not yet experienced. For a while they still traversed the tea estates, and then the mountains enfolded them with deep misty valleys and pyramid shaped peaks, later a plateau, or a *murg*, whose shoulders were clad in dark green juniper and rhododendron, and then rolling country with mountains rising in the distance again. There were delicate buttercups on the Horton Plains that surprised Jane in a tropical country, but Joao reminded her that here the mornings could be bitterly cold, that she was no longer in the sleepy lagoon region of Ceylon.

They reached Hatton, then took the road to Laksapana, the foot of the Peak. Here they rested a while, Joao taking out a hamper and thermos of tea that he had had packed.

'You must eat hugely, little one,' he smiled, 'for there is enough for five. Also' – as Jane protested – 'before you there is a climb of eight steep miles.' He poured the tea and handed it to her.

'It is important that you know of Sri Pada before you pay homage. Tell me how much is in that funny little head.'

Jane wondered whether he would have spoken so

amusedly to a beautiful flame-gold head, but she was lit with interest in Sri Pada and had no objection to conceding to his request.

'It is venerated by Buddhists, Hindus, Muslims and Christians,' she answered. 'On the summit is a great boulder in which there is a footprint-shaped depression.'

'You are a good student,' nodded Joao. 'You would know also that the Buddhists believe it is the mark of Buddha, the Hindus the mark of Siva, the Muslims the footprint of Adam.'

As they ate and drank a family began the quest. They travelled slowly, for there was a cripple among them. Though Jane and Joao lost sight of them in a turn of the track they heard their voices raised in '*Saddhu! . . . Saddhu! . . .*' which Joao said was Hallelujah.

'You can see now,' said Joao, 'it is not just a climb but an exaltation. It is a brotherhood. It could be done by a hardy hiker in commendable time, but that would not be the purpose.'

'I didn't come for a record,' offered Jane soberly. 'I came for that human understanding, for it must be, mustn't it, for Buddhist, Hindu, Muslim and Christian all to climb the same height.'

'Such a wise brown head,' he said back, 'such an understanding brown wren.'

In surprise Jane asked, 'How did you know I was called—' then stopped and flushed.

'Mr. Marsden told me,' replied the senhor.

'Terry? But—'

'We were speaking of home. I expect you could call our conversation Home Thoughts from Abroad. Because you were a brown wren you entered our mutual thoughts. Entered quite nostalgically.' The senhor smiled.

'Nostalgia?' she questioned.

'In Portugal, as in Mr. Marsden's England, we have such small brown birds. Here in Ceylon the bird life is different, here are bold, strident birds, clever, cunning birds, gorgeous blue kingfishers, big fan-tailed pheasants, splendid, colourful creatures one and all, but no small sweet wren.

'Well, little brown bird, are you ready to fly?'

'I suppose,' smiled Jane, 'flying would be much easier, but not, I think, the same deep satisfaction.'

'You have understanding,' he said gravely, and helped her out of the car.

Climbing from the Hatton side, Joao told Jane, there were no dangers and only some three and a half thousand feet to conquer. From the other side, from the valleys of Ratnapura, the ascent was from sea level and much more severe.

That it was not to be easy, though, Jane found in the first few yards. The climb was uncomprisingly steep; it simply went up and up.

'A normally strong walker could reach the summit in three hours,' said Joao. 'I thought we would allow four, then half of that for the descent.'

Almost at each step Jane found the air growing cooler in spite of her warm efforts, in spite of a blazing sun. She saw that the nature of the terrain was changing to wilder grandeur, tremendous boulders flung around, deep gorges suddenly at one's feet, lush jungle growth and huge trailing creepers.

They stopped for a breather, silent for a while in the strange beauty of it all.

'Even April would have appreciated this.' Jane said without thinking, then clapped her hand over her mouth.

'It is all right, little one,' smiled Joao, 'I understand. Your sister indeed would have appreciated it, for it is said that none can stand on the summit without worship in his soul, and Miss Winthrop is intrinsically a fine as well as an exceedingly beautiful woman.'

'Yes, senhor,' Jane said a little unwillingly, hating herself for her lack of alacrity, wondering at her sudden heaviness.

Joao Camoes leaned across and pulled a stem of grass which he peeled then bit into with his strong white teeth.

'I love her.' He said it reflectively . . . to himself . . . but Jane heard.

Suddenly the beauty around her was not there any more, only a blank hollowness bordering on utter despair. The peace was unpeaceful. Nothing was right. What is the matter with me? her heart cried out.

You know, her heart cried back.

Yes, she knew. Unbidden, uninvited . . . even unwanted, her heart had reached out to this big, rather aloof, rather arrogant man. Why, I love him, she knew. I love the man my sister intends to marry. I love the man who intends to marry my sister, he must intend that, for he has just said, and I have heard it: 'I love her.'

'Senhorita, you are suddenly quiet.' The senhor's voice broke into a pain that Jane had never experienced before. She looked up at him. He seemed no different, no more emotional than he had been when he was driving the car. And yet he had just said of April: 'I love her.'

Obviously he had believed he spoke only to himself, for there was not the least glimpse of embarrassment, of an emotion admitted, in his smooth olive face.

The only thing to do, knew Jane, was to be as smooth back to him. He must not know she had heard his thoughts.

'It's this place,' she offered, and he accepted that.

'Yes, it is silencing. If you are rested, shall we go on?'

Jane went heavily for a while, but soon, like all those who climbed these heights, she found her own thoughts slipping away from her, something finer . . . that exaltation Joao had spoken about? . . . taking its place.

The path now was stepped with granite, but the steps were steep, they went ruthlessly up. The trees were thinning away, but the impact of the sun was lessened by the refreshing air.

They passed a nun battling bravely up, a devout Sinhalese calling out pious ejaculations at the steepness ... or Joao assured Jane that they were pious.

But when they reached the little family that had begun the climb as they sat in the car, the father helping a crippled parent, the mother holding the hand of a child, Jane caught at Joao's arm.

'No,' she begged.

'What, senhorita?'

Jane flushed. 'It's not the place to shoulder others aside. It's – it's—'

'I am glad you have said that.' He was looking at her with deep eyes. 'You mean,' he went on, 'it is reverence, unselfishness, consideration, fortitude.

'Yes, senhor.'

'And you mean also that we proceed behind this little unit, that we help them, not go ahead.'

'Yes, senhor.'

'Then we shall do that. Only—' He paused.

'Yes?'

'It will make us late. Very late.'

'Does it matter?'

He smiled back at her. 'That is the answer I wanted.'

Now the steps were really demanding. Jane knew by the strained faces of the pilgrims, none of them robust, that they found the last lap of the climb almost torture. On an impulse she took the weary child into her arms. At the same moment Joao took the elderly cripple in his.

The look on the faces of the man and wife was reward enough without the shower of words.

At that moment there was the clang of a bell above them, and its resonance gave them all new strength.

'A prilgrim has reached the top,' Joao smiled.

'*Saddhu!*' called the little party.

An hour later, which was extremely slow going, but they could travel no faster with the handicapped and the child, they climbed to the Peak, clanged the bell, passed by the holy footprint, stood at last on the summit.

It was as superb a vista as Jane had anticipated, probably, suggested Joao, because everything fell away so quickly and sharply, leaving nothing else to absorb the eye. Beneath them an immense, undulating carpet of earth spread itself out, parts here and there enveloped in eddies of fog.

It was not the hour, the senhor said regretfully, for the fabled Shadow of the Peak, a freak of nature at sunrise when the cone of darkness shortened rapidly, but Jane had no time for regret, she simply stood suffced, rewarded.

'Well, child,' the senhor was consulting his watch, 'even though you said you did not mind being late we must start down again.'

'Descending will be easy,' returned Jane.

But she was wrong – tremblingly wrong. Her knees shook, in fact quite frequently they threatened to give way altogether. The bottom seemed to reach up for her.

'Steady,' said the senhor, and she was grateful for his hand.

Down at last, they went thankfully to the car to sit a long exhausted while before Joao Camoes once more took out the hamper. It was not until he was packing the food away that he said quite casually, 'We will not of course return to Ambanta tonight.'

'Why?' she asked in surprise.

'You will find the rest-houses exceedingly comfortable, if simple.'

'What do you mean?'

The note in her voice must have reached him, for he turned puzzled eyes on her.

'But you distinctly said,' he reminded her, 'when I

warned you we would be late if we delayed that it did not matter.'

'I know, but I didn't think, I mean—'

'What did you mean, senhorita?' The voice was stiff now, uncompromising.

'I thought you – you just meant we would be late getting home.'

'So we would. A night later. We would arrive the following morning.'

'Oh, no!' It was more a little cry than a spoken word.

The senhor's brows were one black line. 'What is this, Miss Winter?' he asked. 'You tell me yes, we will not hurry, but now you sing a different tune.'

'I don't sing any tune at all,' said Jane a little frantically, 'except that I want to get back.'

'Your objection, please?'

'Isn't it obvious?'

'No, it is not. For a Portuguese young woman, to any similar young woman cluttered up with convention and rules a thousand years ago, yes, but you are not one of those. Your country is new, unfettered, fresh.'

'We still,' said Jane with restraint, 'concede to certain standards.'

'Like?'

'Like not – well—'

'Sheltering in a rest-house with an attendant hand maid, attendant room maid, attendant bath maid, attendant clothes maid . . . oh, I could go on and on. But I will not. I will just assure you, senhorita, that we do not camp overnight, as Australians camp, I believe, in any old tent.'

'Then you're misinformed.' Jane's voice was cold. But her hands were hot – hot and trembling. She must not stop. She knew that. It was not just the knowledge of April's wrath, though that was cause enough, it was – it was something else. *She must not be near this man more than she could help.*

He was looking at her with kinder eyes now. When he spoke she saw that he was under the misapprehension that, childlike, she had been labouring under a wrong impression, but now was convinced, and happy to be advised by him.

'It would be too much for you to return tonight, little one. To tell you the truth I myself would not relish the journey back over the range.'

'All the same, that is what we will do.'

Her voice was absolutely calm, and she marvelled at it. How could it be calm with this trembling inside of her?

He was looking at her incredulously, with utter disbelief. Then the look was altering, a shuttered, withdrawn expression taking its place. Of course he would feel like that, she thought wretchedly. Of all the circumspect, prudent people in the world, this man would be the most circumspect, the most prudent. Propriety to him would be a second skin.

Yet I have questioned that in him. I – I have shamed him. Her cheeks burned.

He said nothing, however. He said absolutely nothing all those long hours, those long miles home to Ambanta, the dark ranges slipping past them, all the hazards of the mountainous journey magnified in the blackness of night.

Now Jane knew she had been a fool. It had been dangerous to return like this, and he had known it, but because of a stubborn, wretched girl—

'I'm sorry.' She said it once as he swore softly at some hidden hindrance in the dark that dangerously rocked the car. Still he did not reply.

They did not stop for rest or refreshment, they went grimly, relentlessly on.

Cramped, unbearably tired, thirsty, hungry, Jane longed to cry out to him, but she resisted. If he could resist, she could. After all, it was entirely her fault, she had brought about all this. She must have dozed at the end, for opening her eyes after she had shut them for a minute, or so she had thought, at a particularly hazardous stretch, she saw that they were out of the mountains and once more in the tea country. Half an hour later the familiar plantains of the Ambanta drive were enclosing them. They were home.

It was into the small hours of the morning. Jane, looking sleepily at her watch but not registering the exact time, saw that.

The household, she thought, would all be in bed long ago. But, climbing to the patio, opening the door and going down the long hall, they passed the lighted room, there was wine on the low table, chairs drawn up. April was laughing as Jane had never heard her laugh before . . . gay, caught up with mirth, outside of herself.

Rodriguez was not there. He must have still been ill and gone to bed.

Terry sat there. The room was filled with smoke, and filled with their happy relaxation. Jane could feel the relaxation almost as if it was spelled out to her. But, she thought stupidly, applied jointly to Terry and April, it just didn't make sense.

Still, April was like that. If she was bored, she would fill in time just to relieve the boredom. That was what Jeff had been, simply a relief from boredom. That was what Terry was being now.

With Joao she entered the room. At once the atmosphere changed. April's mood clouded over like the eddies of mist below Adam's Peak. Considering the displeasure Jane had anticipated if she did not return, the displeasure now that she had returned was quite unnerving. Why was April so unmistakably shaken? so annoyed?

It was more obvious again after the girls, bidding good night, went to their rooms.

'Why did you have to come back just then, you little fool?' snapped April, incensed.

'I didn't think you'd like it if I didn't come back.'

'I wouldn't have had a moment of speculation. Not with you. Oh, this is awful! What will Joao think? What could it lead to?'

'You should have thought of that before.' Jane's voice was cold. Really, April was going too far.

'Yes, I should.' April stood quite still in the middle of the room. 'I must have been mad! I dislike him. I dislike everything about him.'

'About Senhor Camoes?'

'Jane, you idiot, *him*! Marsden. And yet ... and yet ... Oh, I must have been fed-up. That was it, sheer ennui. All the same ... all the same *that man must go*. Otherwise,' April continued, an almost hysterical note in her voice now, 'otherwise I – I—'

Wheeling sharply, she went through the communicating door to her own room.

CHAPTER EIGHT

From that moment on there was no deviation on April's part in her drive to be rid of Terry Marsden.

Shrewdly, insidiously, she used every trick up her sleeve, and April had many such tricks, to belittle him in Joao Camoes' eyes. She found him out wrong, rude, tactless, overbearing, indeed, the very antithesis of a welcome guest. When Joao shrugged these failings off as just that, failings, she cloistered herself with Joao in his study so long that Terry in his turn shrugged and told Jane he'd better begin packing.

'But why?' she asked.

'The writing's on the wall, young Jane. Camoes, being the polite fellow he is, won't actually kick me out, he'll suggest I find a greater degree of peace and quiet for my writing elsewhere.'

And that was exactly what happened.

Over sundowners on the terrace that evening Joao said to Terry, 'The Lalanda house over the other side of the hill is vacant, Marsden, while the Reynolds are in Hong Kong for a spot of shopping. I know they would like someone there as a protection, and I thought what an excellent opportunity it would be for you to have some real peace and quiet for your work.'

Terry's I-told-you-so glance at Jane came at the same time as his glib, 'Why, thank you, Joao, Miss Winthrop's chatter certainly was undermining my output.'

If he expected to bait April into a sharp rejoinder he was unsuccessful, she just played with the long cool drink she held with her delicate hands and gave him a stare as frosty as her frosted glass.

But Jane was indignant for Terry. He was being victimized, and she told April so.

'Keep out of this, Jane. If ever I knew what I was doing I know now.'

'I'll go to Senhor Camoes and tell him what I think, April.'

'Go by all means. But I think you'll get a shock.'

'You mean . . .' Did she mean that the senhor had spoken *to* her in the same way as he had spoken *of* her to Jane on their way to Sri Pada? Did she mean he had not said 'I love her' but 'I love you'?

It all made sense. If he had, naturally he would want to be rid of Terry Marsden, if not on his own account then certainly on April's, for when one loved one could not do enough for the loved.

'Go,' flung April triumphantly, 'go and ask Joao for your answer!'

And suddenly driven to it by an urgency of her own, Jane did.

He was walking around the garden, an extremely beautiful garden, for as well as cool air to encourage the more delicate flowers, there were numerous butterflies . . . Ceylon had more than its share of these glorious things . . . the magnificent black and yellow Darsius, the cobalt blue Parinda, many other diaphanous wings.

'It is said,' said the senhor as Jane approached, 'that once a year flimsy legions of these wend their way to Sri Pada to die. It could be true, for I have seen the hordes on their fluttering way myself, and a butterfly always flies to his greatest height before death.' He must have been in a whimsical mood, for he went on, 'And yet so easy not to die, senhorita.

> 'He who has seen a white crow,
>   The nest of a paddy bird,
>   A straight coconut tree,
>   Or a dead monkey,
>   Will live for ever.'

By the dead monkey is meant a monkey who has died. It must happen, but where?

'That,' he concluded with a smile, 'is a very old Sinhalese village saying.'

She could have listened ... and listened. She was always fascinated when he talked like this. But there was something she had to say herself.

'Senhor—' she began.

'No, little one, I will not find you the nest of a paddy bird.'

'*Senhor!*'

He saw the intent in her face and stopped his bantering.

'What, Miss Winter?'

'Mr. – Mr. Marsden,' she stammered.

'What of the gentleman?'

'You're sending him away.'

Coldly he said, 'I have never been so discourteous to a guest.'

'Not in actual words, but in intent.'

'In that either. Really, Miss Winter, you are being very discourteous yourself.'

'Then I'm not sorry. I was very upset this evening to see how Terry was being cast out.'

'You call being provided a more suitable workshop being cast out?'

'That was only the veneer,' she flung. 'Actually you were ridding yourself of him. Or' – as an afterthought – 'ridding April.'

'You are very interested in Mr. Marsden, senhorita,' he said keenly. 'Do you think that is wise?'

'I'm not interested in him – I mean not in the way you imply.'

'Did I imply? It was unintentional.'

She ignored that. She concluded, 'Anyway, even if I am interested it's of no business of yours.'

162

Swiftly he came back, 'On the contrary, it is of very real interest. For two definite reasons.'

'Your own and April's,' she said with more bitterness than she had known was in her. She was surprised at the extent of the bitterness ... but more surprised still at the small smile that all at once twisted his long, sensitive mouth. He seemed somehow pleased. But of course he would be pleased, pleased at being coupled with her half sister. Had he not said: 'I love her'?

All the same she had expected a fairer attitude than this from the senhor, for whatever he was he was always strictly fair. But April's assurance had had firm ground. Whatever Joao Camoes had said to her when they had been cloistered together in his study had been sufficient for April to toss triumphantly, 'Go by all means ... you will receive a shock.'

It hadn't been a shock, though, for she had known before. But it had been ... and turning blindly away Jane felt it sharply ... a hurt.

'Senhorita ... Miss Winter!' His voice followed her as she hurried through the clusters of flowers. 'Jane!'

That nearly halted her, but only nearly. Why not Jane? she told herself. You can't keep on calling your sister-in-law senhorita or Miss Winter.

Your *sister-in-law*. ...

'Well?' April's eyes were snapping. 'Wasn't I right? Doesn't he want the fellow to go?'

'You were right. He wants him to go. But it isn't fair.'

'All's fair,' laughed April, 'in love and war.' Her laugh was a little hollow, though, even for a rather hollow girl like April.

Terry gathered his things, got out his absurd red road-ster, waved an impudent good-bye and went thundering much too fast down the road, then along a 'cart track' to the Reynolds' empty house.

'Good riddance,' said April.

It was all to much for Jane. Suddenly she knew she had had her fill. April no longer needed her, she had established herself, she had found her place. In short it was all over bar the shouting, and Jane shrank from being around when the time came for the shouting. She decided she would move out, either on to England ... fortunately she still held a little money, for April had not needed, not under her pampered circumstances, to call upon her sister as Jane had anticipated ... or back to Australia.

But first she must let her mother know, tell her that she had done everything she had come to do, and now she was bowing out.

Without telling April she wrote the letter, then she asked one of the Tamil boys how one went about posting it. He talked a lot and made a lot of gestures that left Jane none the wiser, and into the conversation came Joao Camoes.

She heard the Tamil explain, 'Missy ask "*Thapal Kanthoruwa Koleda?*"' then heard Joao say, 'So she wants the post office. I'll attend to this.'

After the boy had gone he said, 'There is none here. We have to take mail to the nearest depot, which is rather a distance away.'

'I can't wait very long,' Jane explained.

The brows had risen in the old manner.

'So urgent? And yet you told me this was a wholehearted journey, that you had left nobody behind.'

'My mother.' Jane's own voice was infinitely cool.

'Ah, that is very different. We must of course take your letter to the depot.'

'And take it urgently,' added Jane. 'I'm in a hurry.'

'A hurry, Miss Winter?'

'To leave here. Also although I'm Australian, senhor, I still would like my mother to know my plans.' Her voice reminded him sharply of the few comparisons he had drawn between the young of the two nations.

'I expect,' he accepted mildly, 'I deserve that jibe. We will not take your letter to the depot after all, we will take it to a private airfield I know, who in turn will take it quickly to the Colombo airfield for instant despatch to your home.'

'Thank you, senhor.' Jane turned away.

'You will come with me to this private airfield?' he invited.

'Thank you, no.'

'It is an interesting drive.'

'I said no,' she said stiffly.

He gave a stiff acknowledgment and pocketed her letter. She went and sat on the patio with a magazine waiting for the sound of his car as he went down the drive of plantains with the letter.

When an hour went past and there was no departing car, she got up to demand a reason why her letter had not gone. But her reason came from April, not the senhor.

Typical of April, April who never shrank from doing the most unheard-of things, her sister was sitting on the bed with Jane's *opened* letter in her hand.

'April!' gasped Jane.

'Oh, yes, I know it's dreadful of me, but when Joao told me you had an urgent letter to send and perhaps I, too, had written something which could go at the same time, I got your letter from him ... it doesn't matter how, I just got it ... and here I am, doing the impossible, reading someone else's words. Sorry, pet, but it had to be. You see, this letter's not going.'

'What?'

'Because you're not going. Jane, you just can't leave me.'

'But why, *why*? You've got what you want.'

'Not actually. Not yet.'

'Near enough, then.'

'It isn't. It won't be until . . . until . . . Look, you mustn't go, it – it wouldn't be correct.'

'You talking about being correct!' Jane could not believe it, not in April. 'Anyway,' she reminded her, 'Rodriguez is here to make a third.'

'A third isn't worrying me, a fourth is. And that's what it would be with you gone.'

'April, what are you talking about?'

'Terry.'

'But he's left.'

'Only as far as the other side of the hill. Look, if you can't see what I'm getting at, then I can't make you see, but please, even if it's blindly and without comprehension, stay on and help me, Jane.'

'Help you?'

'Help me not to – not to— Oh, just help me. Please, Jane. Please, wren.'

Jane stood in an agony of indecision. Everything in her called, no, *shouted*, for her to go, but that look in April's face, a look she had never known before, not at any time, under any circumstance, halted her.

'Oh, April,' she said weakly.

'Don't leave me yet, Jane. Promise. Promise!'

'I feel I must get away.'

'Promise!'

A minute of unhappiness, of unease . . . of prescience. Then: 'I promise,' Jane said wearily.

She went outside to the patio again and sank down on the nearest chair. She felt suddenly terribly tired.

When the rest of the household gathered that evening for sundowners . . . the chair in which Terry had always impudently squatted back to front empty for the second night and apparently nobody noticing him gone but Jane . . . Joao Camoes said, 'Tomorrow evening at this time, instead of taking long drinks I intend, with good fortune, that we shall all take a long look.'

'What do you mean, Joao?' asked April in the enthralled voice that, through repetition, was becoming second nature with her whenever it was the senhor to whom she spoke.

'We are going to lie by a water-hole. I have been observing for some time a likely source, a quite large indent of water in an outcrop of gneiss down the valley. The weather has been very dry of late, so the animals have to look further for their supply than their customary source. This appears to me the supply they have found, for I have examined the spot closely and observed several tracks.'

Jane sat almost breathless with the anticipation of it all, to lie low and watch the wild animals come to water stirred her deeply even before it happened. But, remembering how she felt about Senhor Camoes, she determined stubbornly, in spite of a longing to anticipate, not to go. So instead of voicing her pleasure with the others . . . how well April did that pleasure when Jane well knew that all she really felt was distaste . . . she remained stiff and silent.

The drinks came and were drunk. The shadows of night began to fall, and April, and after her Rodriguez, got up to go indoors to dress for dinner.

Jane rose, too.

'Senhorita!' Joao Camoes' voice stopped her.

'Senhor?'

'You did not join in the chorus of enthusiasm just now.'

'For a reason – I'm not enthusiastic. And' – at a look in his face – 'I'm not going.'

'Oh, yes, indeed you are. I let you have your way the other day when you refused to come with me to the airfield, but this is one occasion on which I insist.'

'And one in which I desist.'

'Senhorita, you are still coming, believe me. It is something that no one should miss, given the opportunity, and most particularly you.'

167

'Why should I be singled out?'

'Because there is something deep and clear in you, something that wants to know and feel and experience and learn. You desire to see these animals watering. Admit it, now.'

She could not deny it, so she did not attempt it. Instead she said without any attempt of adornment: 'I do not wish to see them with you.'

'Thank you for your candour at least. I like it better than your evasions. However, seeing there is no one else to conduct you down there, I shall.'

'I shan't go,' she insisted.

'You will cut off your nose to spite your face? See, I have the English clichés.'

'If you mean will I deprive myself, then yes.'

'But you won't,' he replied quite calmly. 'You will come. You will come, senhorita, if I carry you every step of the way. There will be no need to gag you, for once you are there the magic of it all will take your breath away. See, your eyes already are shining. You *long* to come. Why are you stubborn like this?'

'Because I won't be ordered. Just because you're Portuguese—'

'Aren't you forgetting something?' he came in quickly. 'Aren't you forgetting that although I related to you the Sinhalese male superiority, I did not say the same of my own race. Indeed I said, senhorita, that in my country we prefer the man, the woman, to meet half-way. Will you meet me half-way in this?' His smile all at once was quite disarming. He could climb down when he wanted to, she thought grudgingly, this big, arrogant man.

Disarmed in spite of herself, Jane dared, 'And if I don't?'

'Then,' he said, 'I will come all the way to you.' As she went to the door he added softly, 'A promise, Miss Winter, not a threat.'

She could not help becoming excited every time she thought of what lay ahead. It would be an experience, she knew, not given to many, but it was not that special fact that gave her the thrall, it was the pre-knowledge that she would be so near to nature that every vestige of veneer would be stipped from her, she would feel elemental, primeval, at the very beginning of things. Because of this, she listened keenly to Joao's directions the next day, issued at the breakfast table to April, Rodriguez and Jane.

'Once you have taken up your position down there, which must be a safe time ahead of the expected watering, there must be absolute silence. No talk of any sort. Also, bites or strings or scratches from bushes must be borne without even the slightest movement or protest. No brush, no slap, no cough, no sneeze.'

April was fidgeting. Several times she darted an appealing look at Rodriguez. He and his food poisoning had got her out of the ordeal of the climb to Adam's Peak; could Roddy again find an escape?

But Rodriguez's eyes were sparkling, he was as keen as Joao. 'We will take our guns?' he asked.

'Only in case protection is needed. To shoot an animal who comes down to drink is murder. By the way, ladies, no insect repellent – animals are sensitive to strange scents. And no perfumes or powders.'

'Really, Joao!' pouted April.

'To my way of thinking you do not need them at any time.' Joao made a gallant gesture, to which April responded with a soft smile.

She was not so amiable, though, after he went out to the estate, taking Rodriguez with him, though even had the younger man remained Jane doubted if April could have prevailed upon him to think out an escape. He was looking forward to the afternoon as much as April was dreading it.

'Not even insect repellent! I'll be covered with blotches. And I look awful without any make-up at all.'

'I think you'd better wear your jodphurs,' advised Jane to keep her from dwelling on the unhappy ultimatum. 'It could become chilly.'

'Just to see some old bear or something!'

A bear! Jane felt her blood tingle.

Late in the afternoon, but well before the first faint shades of evening, the four started down the narrow track to the valley of Joao's choice. At the very bottom and along no track at all now they forced their way through coiling vines and rotted trunks, keeping an eye out for snakes, to a platform, or mesa, that the senhor had had built in the branches of a tree. There they climbed, one after the other, stretched out on their stomachs, then that was that.

At least that was what April's sulky eyes telegraphed to Jane. These mosquitoes, said the turquoise eyes. The hardness of the boards on your limbs. That branch that's scratching my head.

But Jane could not return the look; she was in a seventh heaven.

Almost at once a family of monkeys had come, too, to watch ... later she was to be told that monkeys enjoyed watching water-holes as much as human beings. It was delightful to observe their antics ... alert when they believed an animal was approaching, bored to the extent of tantalizing each other when nothing eventuated.

Then ... a faint stir in Rodriguez beside Jane ... something *was* happening. Jane held her breath in thrall.

A sambhur, or variety of deer. A huge, noble fellow with fine antlers and a splendid stance. Hardly had he gone than a Ceylon bear came along, smallish, rather scruffy and very nervy. He drank quickly, then disappeared. The buffalo some half hour later not only drank he immersed himself, wallowing until Jane feared no other animal would care to drink from the muddied depths.

But the hole soon cleared after he had lumbered off, and even if it had not, by the time they received their next visitor it would have had time, had rain fallen, to refill. For they were to lay prone and waiting for almost two more hours.

At the end of the hours even Jane's previously unprotesting limbs were protesting. April, at the end of her tether at last, not caring any more, sat up.

At the same moment the Ceylon leopard, with no perceptible movement or approach, reached the waterhole, stood a poised moment in lithe beauty, then, though not dangerous to man under ordinary circumstances, alarmed by April's movement, leaped up instinctively before it leapt instinctively away and into the jungle again.

But it was the upward leap that did the damage. The enormous spring missed April, missed Joao, missed Rodriguez, but caught Jane's arm. It was only a glancing blow, but the pain was all-encasing. Jane felt the red-hot sear of it, gave what she believed was a cry but was only a small sigh, then knew no more.

When she opened her eyes it was hours later and she was in bed back at the bungalow. April sat at the side of the bed, her eyes worried. The doctor who had attended Rodriguez for his food poisoning waited beside April. Rodriguez sat on the left. And at the foot, so pale she did not recognize him at first, stood Joao.

CHAPTER NINE

JANE'S consciousness did not last long.

Barely had the weaving faces around her taken shape, began to belong instead of to nebulous people to people she knew, than the mists rolled in again, enfolded her in unawareness and unreality. She seemed weighed down with lead, though at times she felt herself soaring lighter than air. On these occasions she realized rather drunkenly that the sedative, or whatever it was the doctor had given her, must be wearing off, for she was dimly conscious of pain, and she saw people again.

She saw Joao. Always she saw Joao.

Sometimes it would be April who was with him, sometimes Rodriguez, and once, she recognized him even in her muzziness, it was Terry. But every time her heavy lids opened, the Senhor as well was there.

At length there came a time when the lids were less heavy and they stayed open.

The doctor examined her again, re-dressed the arm.

'I'm not having any more drugs,' protested Jane.

A very charming Sinhalese, trained, he told her, in Australia under the Colombo Plan, he smiled back and promised to insert no more needles.

'Unless,' he added, 'the arm needs it. As for shock, you haven't any.'

'The arm is sore, but not that bad.'

'Nonetheless it will need close attention. In a tropical country like Ceylon, infection can come very rapidly. I could wish, for all that I was desperately homesick when I wintered there for my warmer birthplace, that it was July in Melbourne.'

Joao Camoes had entered silently, and his eyes glinted keenly.

'No wishing that now,' he put in, 'for it is summer during this month in Australia. But' – a pause – 'it is winter in Albufiera.'

'Albufiera?' Jane and the doctor asked together.

'*My* birthplace.' He smiled and bowed. He made the usual polite interchanges that visitors do with patients, insisted that Jane ask for anything she required, then told the doctor he would see him on his way out.

Terry came along, his smile, thought Jane gratefully, as good as a tonic. She would never know, laughing weakly at a ridiculous joke, why April did not like him.

'Well, Janey,' he grinned, 'the leopard incident might have put you to bed, but it at least got me back into the house.'

'Are you back?' she asked.

'No. But I was on the night they brought you up from the jungle. There's no grapevines in Ambanta, but the news spread just the same. The word that Missy had been savaged brought me breaking all speed limits to be here to write up the scene at the deathbed.'

'And I disappointed you!'

'You did, as a matter of fact. I thought it was April. I had a very smug feeling in me when I thought of looking down on that girl instead of her looking down on me. But' – a shrug – 'it was you instead.'

'Still busy on the tea articles, Terry?'

'Yes, but not so busy that I can't do a piece on "The day I looked into a leopard's eyes." Though' – regretfully – 'being a woman of letters yourself probably you've reserved all the rights.'

'No,' admitted Jane, 'I haven't. I've never written very seriously. In fact' – ruefully – 'you could call me rather lackadaisical. I'm not ambitious, Terry.'

He did not answer for a while, which was unlike the

voluble journalist, then when he did he said, rather oddly, or so Jane thought, 'That's good, kid. In my book that, in a woman, is my pipe dream.'

He did not stop long after that. He planted a light affectionate kiss on Jane's brow, then left.

Rodriguez came in. He was a little excited, but evidently he had been told not to divulge the cause of his excitement, for he kept strictly to the same visitor-patient patter that Joao had.

At length, tired of trivialities, Jane asked, 'What happened to the leopard?'

'Dear Jane, don't upset yourself.'

'I'm not upset ... but I would be if I thought it had been shot. It couldn't help doing what it did, it was alarmed.'

'It was not shot, it ran into the jungle. As far as being shot – well, it's extremely unlikely it will water there again even if we placed a posse. Which, of course, Joao would not countenance. He's very keen on wild life, though I must say' – a sigh – 'it, or Ceylon, is not to my liking. However—' His eyes brightened and he wet his lips as though to make a statement. But, on second thoughts, he did not. He, too, kissed Jane lightly and went out.

The doctor came again. The nurse.

When, thought Jane a little crossly, is April coming? But it was not until early evening that her sister finally visited her. Jane was sitting up now, feeling, apart from a stiffness and a rawness in her arm, quite fit.

April perched on the side of the bed and said at once in a breathless little voice, 'Jane, we're going to Portugal.'

'What? April, are you ill yourself? You look very flushed.'

'It's excitement. It's happening at last!'

'What is?'

'Joao has arranged a private charter for the four of us

to leave, the doctor permitting, and his last examination said that you were definitely sufficiently fit, for the Algarve.

'The Algarve is a Portuguese province, darling, down in the bottom corner.' That was typical of April, no points of the compass for that lovely flaming head. 'The capital is Faro — fruit, fishing, wine, salt. Her voice was unnaturally high and it held a note slightly bordering on hysteria. 'But it's Albufiera we're going to.'

'That's the senhor's birthplace,' recalled Jane.

'Yes. Actually his *palacio* ... yes, Jane, it's what it sounds, a palace ... is back in the hills from there, but he has this beach place where he wants you to recuperate.'

'Me? But I have no need to recuperate. I feel wonderfully fit.'

'A leopard leaps out at you and you feel fit! Don't be ridiculous, Jane.'

'I'm not being ridiculous, I'm being truthful. I have no need to go to Portugal.'

'Then for pity's sake, for my sake, don't say so.'

'What do you mean, April?'

'I mean I must go.'

'Then go.'

'But I can't, can't you see that? I can't go unless you go. It all depends on you, Jane.'

'Why does it depend on me?'

'Because Joao is only going because of you. He has this "thing" that you need further medical attention, and what better medical attention to a Portuguese than the attention in Portugal. I's quiet reasonable when you come to think of it. We would feel the same.

'Very well, then, I'll go back to Australia for my treatment.'

'Jane, you can't!'

'I can. I will. That is, if I have to undergo treatment elsewhere. Anyway I would feel it was a slight to the good Sinhalese doctor, and I wouldn't be a party to it.'

'But that's all settled. The Sinhalese doctor suggested a change of climate himself.'

'But not particularly Portugal.'

'If not, then certainly not Australia, for it's summer there. A cooler, more moderate air, he said, to assist healing.'

'I'm healed.'

'Then, Jane' – April got up from the bed and went to stand at the window in the way she used to – 'do it for me. I have to go. Can't you see?'

'Yes, I can see,' said Jane slowly, 'I can see the whole distasteful design of it all. But what I can't see, April, and I won't, is my part in the wretched thing. I won't help you to clinch your deal. I'm sorry if the words are raw, but that's how I feel.'

'They are raw,' admitted April, 'but it still makes no difference to me. You see I just have to get away from here before – before it's too late. That it happens to be Portugal offering as an escape it just coincidental. I – I mean, Jane, even though that "distasteful design" you just spoke about is pretty true, it's not my real reason. Jane – Jane, can't you see *why* I have to get away?'

'I know.' Jane's voice was stolid.

'No, not that, not that . . . Oh, oh, what's the use?'

Something of the driving panic in her half-sister reached Jane. She looked at her curiously.

'You sound almost as though you're running away from something, but that couldn't be true.'

'No,' said April, 'it couldn't be true.' Her laugh was high and unnatural again. She sat on for a while, but she made no other attempt to persuade her sister.

But when the nurse came . . . a smiling-eyed Low-Country girl with shining black hair caught up in a knot beneath her white veil . . . she left Jane to have her arm

re-dressed, only pausing at the door to look back in silent
entreaty, an appeal that reached across the room to beg
and implore.

It only remained for the senhor to add his piece and he
did so when the nurse had finished.

'More comfortable now?' He had pulled up a chair by
the bedside.

'I'm a fraud. I should be up,' smiled Jane.

'I am glad you feel that well, senhorita, otherwise I
would have had second thoughts on allowing you to fly
tomorrow.'

'Then have second thoughts, senhor, for I am not flying.' Jane paused. 'Not, anyway, to where you have
planned.'

'And where have I planned?'

'Portugal.'

'I see already you have been told.'

'Not told,' persisted Jane stubbornly, 'acquainted.
Acquainted of your plans.'

'You are in the mood to correct. Then I will be, also.
I have made no plans . . . plans are tentative things . . .
I have made definite arrangements. The private small
plane will take us down to Ratmalana airport and from
there we will take a private charter to Lisbon. From there
another small craft to a field very near my home.'

'Is a *palacio* a home?' Jane inserted sharply.

'An Englishman's home is an Englishman's castle,' he
returned evenly. 'I see no reason why that should not be
reversed for a Portuguese. Could not' – he swept her a
look that only for the idea being too ridiculous Jane could
have categorized as appealing, appealing? the senhor?
. . . 'the castle of a Portuguese be his home?'

'It could be, but I won't be finding out.'

'I agree. I have decided that rather will we go to my
cliff house at Albufiera. There the weather will be both
bracing yet temperate.'

'Senhor Camoes,' broke in Jane, 'I am not going at all.'

'But Miss Winter,' he said, still even, 'you are. What happened in the jungle, the leopard incident, lies entirely on my shoulders. Not only the territory was mine but the arrangements for the expedition mine also. Can't you see that I am responsible for you, that I do not *dare* omit the precaution of removing you from Ambanta.'

'Oh!' Jane could not help a certain deflation. 'Then it's really a matter of – of liability.'

He did not answer for a moment. Then he said, 'And something else.'

But he meant some*one* else. Jane knew that. The fact that her injury could be attended at the same time was just something that had happened rather conveniently, since the senhor, being the senhor, would never have taken April home without someone else of her own sex.

And he wanted ... and intended ... to take April home. Had he not said: 'I love her'? *I love her*.

'Senhorita?' His voice broke in, asking for her decision, even though his decision ... for her ... had been made.

Jane made one more attempt.

'I don't like to discard the Sinhalese doctor, he has been very good to me.'

'You will not be discarding him, child. Do you think I would take the risk of changing medicos mid-course? He, of course, will come as well.'

Jane just lay wordless. What else was there to say, to protest?

The small plane took the party down to Ratmalana airport the next morning. As Jane changed crafts she could see working elephants, urged on by mahouts, padding the road down firmly, and she thought how lucky Vasco was in his private valley.

At once the big craft set out, and then it was like the

turning pages of an atlas, the countries beneath them taking the same shape as the remembered shapes in the atlas. Almost, thought Jane, you looked down to pick out the appropriate colours, pink for India, yellow for Persia, just as you had as a child.

Karachi ... Cairo ... briefly at Algiers ... hours of drifting sleepily, waking refreshed, then Lisbon rising up, but no chance to see it, for the next small plane was waiting for the final leg. For that private strip belonging to the Conde de Camoes at Albufiera.

That last, anyway, was what April's glittering eyes were telegraphing to Jane. Once during the journey she had whispered, 'Pinch me, Janey, is all this true? Not only a private plane but a private doctor as well. That man must be positively rolling! And to think I had my ideas on little nephew Roddy!'

'April—' began Jane.

'Darling, I'm beyond being reproached. I am, thank heaven, beyond all that has happened before this moment. I'm safe.'

'Safe?'

But April had only kept glittering.

It was a brief hop to the province of Algarve. The plane made a smooth landing, the party got out and boarded two waiting cars. How well the senhor did things, thought Jane grudgingly, but the smile on her half-sister's face was not grudging, while no doubt, Jane knew, April was not thinking of Joao as the senhor but as the Conde.

They ran swiftly through a forest of eucalyptus that reminded Jane of home.

'Acclimatized, of course,' said the senhor, 'but these cork are our own.'

They passed big imposing gates that Rodriguez said led to the *palacio* ... an *avenida*, or avenue, of magnolia wound round concealingly as far as the eye could see, and though she did not glance at her, Jane could imagine

April's shining eyes. But the *palacio* remained withdrawn from sight, though the cliff house, when it was reached, certainly indicated that the Camoes' main stronghold should be something quite breathtaking, for even the sea-side home was in its way a minor castle.

Even April was silent as she followed Joao down the long corridor, lofty, as most less modern Portuguese buildings are, and given to much fretted oak and baroque.

There was sufficient accommodation for thrice their party, and, as at the bungalow at Ambanta, April and Jane had rooms with communicating doors. The furnishings were purely Portuguese, rich of colour and fabric, nothing airy. But the view through the window dispelled any sense of heaviness, floating blue, the blue of both sea and sky, drifted in until, instead of the rather ponderous reds and burgundys, it became a blue refuge instead. At least a blue refuge it seemed to Jane. She felt at once infinitely at peace here.

But not, surprisingly, April. April stood, brow creased, uncertain, on edge.

'It's all too much,' she said more to herself. 'I can't feel myself think.'

Suddenly touched by her confusion, if not understanding why she was confused, Jane asked gently, 'Do you want to think?'

'No, I don't. Thank you, Janey, for reminding me, keep on doing that, wren. And now shall we unpack?'

Dinner was eaten in a long, high-ceilinged room facing the sea. There was a great fire burning, for it was a cold night. When, during conversation, Joao anticipated doing some swimming in the week they would be here . . . where, then? wondered Jane briefly . . . April gave a little shiver of protest and inquired about icebergs.

'You will be surprised,' Joao smiled, 'at the temperature on the beach compared to that on the cliff. Down there the winter sun shines hotly. You can lie in your bathers and look eighty feet up to people in thick coats.

The meal over, the young doctor took a look at Jane's arm, then having proclaimed his satisfaction at her progress, he suggested that she have an early night.

'For after all' ... a flash of white teeth in a smiling brown face ... 'it has been a journey of many miles.'

To Jane's surprise, for Rodriguez had excused himself and gone out and her sister could have had her Count to herself, April said she would go to bed as well. She even saw Jane into bed, plumped her pillows, then did something she seldom bothered about, she kissed her goodnight.

'Thank you, Janey,' she whispered before she clicked out the light. 'You've helped all you could, it's not your fault that—'

'What is it, April?' Jane sat up, the sudden movement hurting the arm. 'April, is anything wrong?'

'In these surroundings of riches? Don't be foolish, darling.'

'You sounded unhappy.'

'I'm as happy as I deserve.'

'Is that an answer?'

'It's all the answer I can think of. I'm terribly tired, Jane, don't fuss. I'm going to sleep in until ten o'clock in the morning. Roddy told me that it's bitterly cold on the beach until that hour because the sun doesn't get over the cliff. Goodnight, kid.'

But she didn't sleep. Jane, not sleeping either, knew it because she heard her tossing restlessly, once she heard her walking round her room.

Walking to a window again to look out?

But in the morning, none of the household venturing out into the very cold air until after Rodriguez's correct ten o'clock, April was a different person. She was quite enchanted.

Hurrying down to the beach, and shivering with every step, suddenly, like walking out of a refrigerator, it was summer in winter. April, lying back in a brief bikini, stretched luxuriously and with all the grace of a cat.

'But this is wonderful!' she thrilled.

While she and Jane sunbaked, Joao, Rodriguez and the young doctor swam the length of the exceedingly pretty beach. Then they came back to the girls, and the five of them basked, talked desultorily, often slept. It was an idyllic existence, utterly blissful, utterly lazy, and it set the pattern for the week.

Blazing fires at night. Hot sun by day. Always the sough of the sea, and the sight of the steep and picturesque fishing cottages, all in dazzling white but each with a differently designed chimney. Each day followed in the same pattern, though after the third day they were only four, Rodriguez having deserted them for pastimes of his own.

'I must tell you,' smiled the senhor, 'that there was a childhood friend very precious to Rodriguez. Will it disturb you' – to April – 'if I whisper that it was a girl?'

'You can sing it aloud,' April assured him. 'I wish him luck.'

'And I,' put in Jane, 'wish him no return to Ceylon, for he seems happier here.'

'Yes,' nodded Joao, 'and I will have some words about that with my sister. I do not believe she will be difficult. Her only brother being unmarried, I think she was under the misapprehension that I needed Rodriguez out there. But now it is different. I intend not to need to borrow anyone else's family.'

His eyes were closed, so neither April nor Jane could read the dark depths, but their own glances met . . .

The doctor took a run up to Lisbon to inspect the medical university. Rodriguez was away so much they barely saw him, even at meals.

'I think,' shrugged Joao, 'the romance must go well.'

It was that day, the girls having esconced themselves on the beach with rugs, cushions, magazines and the huge hamper that Joao always had brought down, the senhor taking his usual beach-length swim, that Jane, leaning back on the sand and daydreaming, opened her eyes as she always did to enjoy the luxury of seeing people eighty feet up in overcoats, saw – saw—

No, it couldn't be!

She closed her eyes again. But when she opened them once more, with clearer focus, more deliberation, she still saw the figure, and it still looked like—

But now it was gone.

She sat up and unscrewed the thermos. A cup of coffee, she thought. I must be seeing things.

April, a little greenishly pale, though that must be the reflection of the flawless pale blue water on the flawless pale yellow beach, said quickly, 'No, you'll strain your arm. Let me, Jane.' And did – spilling the entire contents on the sand.

'Oh dear, how stupid! Now I must climb up for more.'

'Not for me, April.'

'But certainly for Joao. He looks for a cup when he comes out.'

That was true, but all the same Jane did not think that Joao would make an issue of it if by accident it was not there. Still, if April wanted to do the service, let her climb the eighty feet.

'Please yourself,' she smiled.

'Oh, I am, Jane. Jane, I *am*!' It was an odd rejoinder but one that Jane did not think about. Not then. She watched April climbing up. She watched her out of sight.

Joao came out of the water and rubbed himself dry with an immense towel. Jane explained about the coffee, and he nodded, and they both lay in the sun, and Jane, anyway, slept.

When she awoke the sun was much lower. April was not there, but the thermos was.

'Has she come and gone again?' asked Jane, still a little stupid with sleep.

'No. Just gone.'

'But the flask is here.'

'It never went. I noticed that when I came out of the water. She never took it up.'

'But – but I don't understand. That's what she went for.'

'No, she never went up for that.'

'Joao ...' Jane always addressed him as senhor, but this time a puzzled urgency unloosened her tongue.

If he noticed her use of his name he did not show it. 'Come, little one,' he said, 'come up the cliff to the house. I cannot tell you, for I do not know myself – not yet. I can only think—'

'Think what?'

'What I have observed and sensed and felt.'

'What? *What*?'

'It is not my prerogative to tell you. It is hers.'

'April's?'

'Your sister's, senhorita. Come, and we will see if she has done that thing.'

'*Done* it? Why, you sound as though she won't be there, as though if she has anything to tell it will not be by mouth but by – by—'

'By note. By letter. Yes, and I think it will. Now, can you manage that cushion? I will carry the rest.'

It was useless to try to hurry up to the cliff top. Apart from the rugs, the magazines and the hamper, Jane's arm had to be protected. Today it seemed to the suddenly desperate Jane that the senhor fussed inordinately at each rocky bend, protected her too much.

'We're twice the usual time,' she cried out at last in dismay.

'There is plenty of time,' he assured her. 'A lifetime, I believe.' At least Jane thought it sounded like that.

But at last they were there. Walking the last few steps into the cliff house. Jane was going through the rooms calling April's name. And April was not responding.

A servant spoke in Portuguese to Joao, and Joao nodded soberly.

'Upstairs,' he said to Jane, 'there is a note.'

'A note?'

'For you, senhorita. Senhorita Winthrop left it.'

'Left it?'

'When she left here herself.' With delicacy he asked, 'do you want to read it alone, or shall I come with you?'

Jane stood perfectly still, feeling somehow suspended, weightless, not there or anywhere, outside of herself. But she had to come down to reality. She had to go upstairs and see that April really had gone. Why? Where? And she had to read that note.

'Come with me,' she said jerkily, suddenly very young and wondering and needing help, and, protecting her injured arm, he went with her up the steps.

CHAPTER TEN

'DEAR WREN, I have left for England with Terry Marsden. I'm marrying him tonight. You thought you saw him when you were down on the beach. I knew I saw him, and I knew that I had been waiting only for that.

'I love him, Jane. I did right from the moment I first met him, but I fought it with all my power. I'd had enough of not enough, I wanted to be important and rich.

'I admit none of this is what I planned, or ever would have planned, but it's no use, little sister, it's stronger than I am, and even if Terry and I are poor as church mice we'll be that together, and though it will be hard for you to believe it of me, that's all I care about.

'Don't worry about Mummy throwing a fit, she'll see in Terry and me Father and herself all over again. Remember that love she used to prate and I used to sneer about? But it's true, small Jane, it's true.

'Yet what am I doing telling you and Joao?' – Inserted under this was a man's writing, evidently Terry's. It read: 'What, indeed?'

Then they both had signed: 'April. Terry.'

Jane, still dazed, suspended, weightless, put the letter down. She permitted Joao to lead her to the window-seat, gently press her down.

'It's not true, is it?' she asked vaguely.

'Quite true. I knew it on the sands, I knew it as you slept.'

'Then—'

'Then why didn't I awaken you? What could you have done?

'Stopped them.'

'Stopped a dream? For it is that, child. I have ob-

186

served this pair, reckless, feckless, selfish, unthinking. They were still made for each other, and they will succeed. It is all for the better that April has fought against it, it makes the losing more a triumph, a triumph of love. I believe that Marsden will come good, and very good. He was empty before, purposeless, now he has April to solidify a future that was barely the glimmer of a hope.'

'But April . . .'

'She has him in her turn. That she needs him, and needs him desperately, has been proven in these last weeks. Why, otherwise, did I agree to come here, child? I could see her desperation, her last bid to live her own life, not a life with him.'

'It was not only her own life she was thinking about,' put in Jane tremulously. 'It was – yours as well.'

He smiled carefully. 'Oh, that! First Rodriguez, then me. Do you think for a moment that I—'

But Jane was still worried.

'April can't live like a church mouse, she's not the sort,' she protested.

'*Was* not the sort. She has changed now. She is half a person, and Terry is the other half. Anyway, what is this talk of church mice? He is a fine journalist, and your sister has a quite remarkable voice.'

Jane looked at him in astonishment. 'A voice? But you said . . . you said . . .'

'Of course. As the English – and no doubt the Australians – put it, I played along. April, if the extra money is needed, will be able to earn it. Though I have a feeling that the new April, with Marsden beside her, will be content with less.

'Well, little one, what is the next frown on your brow?'

'Mother,' sighed Jane.

'Your sister has explained that. I don't think you are really worried.'

'No, I'm not. What April does is always right with

Mother. And money has never really concerned Mummy very much.' The unremarkable flat, Jane remembered, the ever-present pack of cards, the living on the past – and her Vernon. Those first happy days. She felt suddenly sorry for her own father. Those who kiss and those who are kissed.

She was not aware that she said that aloud.

'What is it, Jane?' he asked. She told him, and he nodded. 'It is sad, yes, and yet to either it is the next best thing.'

'To loving equally?'

'Yes.'

She thought that over, sad herself. It had to be the next best thing for her. For she loved this man.

But also, she remembered, it had to be the next best thing for him. He loved April. He had said so.

'I'm sorry, Joao,' she sighed.

'Sorry?'

'For you. I – I remember going up to Sri Pada.'

'So do I. How could I forget?'

'You said it then.'

'Said what?'

' "I love her." You – you said it about April.'

'Said it of . . . why, yes, I did. And I meant it. Indeed, I meant it.'

'Poor Joao!'

'Wait, little one, wait. I never finished that day. It should have been "I love her because she brought me you." '

'Brought—' she began.

'You – *you*, Jane. Plain Jane. The little brown wren. I don't know about that, all I know is that every time ever since when I have been with you I have cried *Ayubowen* in my heart and put my hands together in prayer.'

'But, Joao—' she faltered.

'Can't you see, child, you are the one I want to kiss,

and seeing you have nothing to give in return all I can hope is that giving and not receiving can be my next best.'

'But I have it to give, oh, I have, Joao! I just didn't understand ... I never dreamed ... I couldn't dare hope ...'

'But surely I told you, told you a hundred times? A Portuguese, I said, is not a Sinhalese, he comes half-way, and he will come, if needed, and if love is waiting there, all the way to a heart that is whole. You had said your heart was whole.'

'It was.' Jane looked up at him shyly, then, seeing his lean, sensitive face, the face she loved, she said with rising strength, 'But not now. I and my heart are not whole any more.' Slowly, with conviction, with knowledge, 'Not ever any more.'

'For which I say *Ayubowen,* for which I join my finger-tips again.' And Joao did.

Standing in the blue-washed room, they stood all at once instead on Sri Pada ... by the Sacred Footprint ... having clanged the bell of the temple.

Having reached the top.

4 FREE
Harlequin Romances

TAKE THESE 4 *Harlequin Romances* FREE